MONSTERLAND

A Novel

by

Gregory L. Norris

Book Clubs & Special Ordering:

Special discounts are available on quantity purchases by **book clubs,** corporations, associations, and others. For details, contact the publisher at director@vanvelzerpress.com.

Cover design by Trisha Lewis
Edits & Layout & Publishing via Van Velzer Press
Paperback ISBN: 978-1-954253-61-2
Hardback ISBN: 978-1-954253-67-4
Ebook ISBN: 978-1-954253-65-0
Audio ISBN: 978-1-954253-62-9

LCCN Available upon request
director@vanvelzerpress.com

Printed in the United States of America

*To all those wonderful monster movies
and creature double features of my
boyhood that played every Saturday
afternoon on WLVI-Channel 56, this
novel is lovingly dedicated.*

The monsters haven't been hiding under beds for more than a decade.

No, they're now at Monsterland, which occupies seventy-seven acres of former rural farm country where they used to grow strawberries, with another five devoted to parking. At Exit 13, you veer right. Travel past the gas station and mini-mart, beyond a string of ranch houses built in the 1960s, and right again at the sign. You can't miss it. Then you travel down a long country road through a cathedral of towering sap pines, and there it is. You'll see the roller coaster with its steep inclines that loop sharply enough to twist stomachs inside out—the Dragon Express, so named for the design, is one of the deepest plunges of tracks in America. You'll smell the concessions, the best of which is the Monster Grilled Cheese, the park's specialty and made with muenster, of course. It costs as much as a doctor's visit without insurance and is served with a cup of blood-red tomato soup for a few bucks more.

But you'll also *feel* the amusement park on your approach to the main gate, above which several plaster gargoyles gaze down with malevolence through unblinking eyes that light up after sunset. They call that ripple "the Monsterland Hum." It's a wrongness that slithers over your skin, works its way deeper, and rattles around in your bones. The popular belief is that it's the result of the various protections designed to keep the monsters in their exhibits. Some think it's just old-fashioned human instinct warning us to not get any closer—this is a place of monsters after all, and we're not designed to willingly want to be near them. We weren't created to fly, to travel beneath the ocean, or walk on the moon, either. But that's *Homo sapiens* for you—bolder than we were born to be. Or just plain foolish.

Feeling a fool, it was on a deceptively bright April morning that I drove my nine-year-old secondhand ride right off Exit 13 and right again through the long stretch of pinewoods, unemployed and borderline desperate. The signs appeared, designed to draw in families and their vacation dollars, but to me they seemed a warning.

>*See the Vampire Coven!*
>*See the Mummified Terrors From Ancient Egypt!*
>*See the Horrible Sasquatches!*
>*See the Monster, the Living Man Without a Soul*
>>*Made From Stitched-together Body Scraps!*
>*See the Horror From Loch Ness!*
>*See the Giant Monster that Trampled a City Flat!*

I caught sight of the Dragon Express's tracks through a break in the trees, suffered the first tickle over the skin near my throat warning me I was close, and choked down a dry swallow. Suddenly, the button-down shirt over white T, khakis, and wingtips I wore to weddings and funerals all seemed sizes too small, as though my clothes were conspiring to suffocate me. I drove out of the cathedral formed by the trees and saw it in its full and gaudy spectacle—Monsterland, situated behind a mote of chain link fence and brick walls and, no doubt, plenty of protective wards.

And then I saw the other sign, the one that had lured me here.

Job Fair Today From 10-2—Use F-Gate

F-Gate. As I shut off my engine and wondered if it would start again, it struck me how appropriated that designation was. I was F'ed if I didn't get this job.

Times were tough. Not just for me but a lot of people. Inflation, the economy…add in an ugly divorce, and I couldn't recall a time when I'd known things to be tougher. Like a lot of days in recent memory, I went through the motions on a kind of autopilot: through F-Gate to an outdoor waiting pen that already had three dozen other job applicants—I did my best not to think that we'd only been let in as fodder for the vampires and the aquatic horror from Loch Ness—and from there past the outer wall of the mummy exhibit, down a tunnel, and to a conference room with no windows and chairs that were hell on the ass.

Like the chubby young woman with the dark hair and glasses who guided us there, the man waiting in the room to greet us wore a black polo shirt with a cartoon bat embroidered on the upper right chest—the Monsterland logo. I guessed he was in his early to mid-thirties, maybe five years older than I was. He wore a perfect mustache and goatee and flashed a confident, authoritative smile. The slick Monsterland PR bureaucrat's name was Ravi Nakur.

"Welcome to Monsterland," he said and did a rapid headcount—thirty-three, I'd been close. "We've got the need for twenty-four new Monsterlanders, as we like to call our team." He laughed. Those around me did, too. I paid lip service with a chuckle because, as stated, I was on autopilot. I'd gotten that far even though I was already worried it was too far to turn back.

"By the time this interview process is over, I'll be happy if I've filled half our needs. A third. Monsterlanding isn't for everyone. It isn't for the weak of stomach, the weak of spine, or the weak of soul. What you'll find out there—" he tipped his chin in what I imagined was the direction of the nearest attraction. "Let's just say that the monsters are real…and deadly."

Great. And I was here, ready to beg for a job that paid only two bucks more an hour than minimum wage, one in which I'd be required to wear a black polo shirt with a silly cartoon bat on it.

"How many of you are up to this awesome feat?" Ravi challenged more than asked, a smug little smirk displayed.

Hands around me raised without hesitation. I tossed a glance to my right and saw my arm extended up past my head. Foolish, like I said. Pretty damn stupid, in fact.

He showed us historical clips we'd all seen but watched again because it was part of the interview process. The first showed the vampire coven, captured and shackled in silver cuffs, being dragged down attic stairs spitting and with smoke wafting off their bindings.

"That's the Baroness Ursula, presently sleeping the day away half the length of a football field from where we've gathered," Ravi said.

The next video clip took the audience into the deep, dark woods. *"We got one!"* a man was heard shouting off screen as the hand holding the camera nearly dropped it in excitement. "We *(BLEEP)*ing got one!" The jiggled images stabilized enough to show a clearing and a cage, the kind men lower themselves under water in believing they'll be safe from great white sharks stirred into a feeding frenzy. This prison had dropped a hirsute giant legend into the modern landscape, one with wide, angry eyes that threw itself at the bars and threatened to topple the cage. The captured beast emitted a wild animal's cry that was nearly musical in its timbre.

"We currently boast *four* sasquatches here at Monsterland," Ravi said. It sounded like more PR that had been practiced to death.

Another video played. Now we were looking at a rainy cityscape, which could only mean one thing: Cleveland, eleven years earlier, when the Great Lakes Monster had come striding out of the murk and leveled a goodly part of the downtown. There was no mistaking that footage, and I didn't. The room fell silent. The air grew heavy and harder to breathe.

There it stood upright on two powerful legs, its armored reptilian hide of scales colored platinum in the overcast. It tossed back its head and let forth with a blood-freezing roar that smothered the soundtrack of police sirens and human screams. From there, the clip followed the monster's progress until it tromped closer, the pounding of its steps like terrible thunder. The visuals vanished into crackles of static, which, we all knew, had signaled the cameraman's death. The video, recorded on a cell phone, had been recovered after one well-placed sidewinder missile launched from a fighter jet had blasted through the monster's ribcage and out the other side of its chest.

"And you all know about our first and most famous attraction, the OG of monsters, the Great Lakester," Ravi said after pausing the show. "The investors cut a deal for its corpse. Built the giant tank on these very grounds, and nearly went bankrupt filling it with formaldehyde."

Another laugh from Ravi, followed by the same from the audience. I shifted on that miserable chair, sucked in air, grew aware of the dampness under my armpits, and, more so, the unpleasant tickle that had worked beneath my skin and into my marrow.

"Now why would anyone choose to work at a theme park built around genuine, honest-to-*badness* monsters?" Ravi asked, again his question a challenge.

"Because I grew up on horror movies," a fresh-faced young man among the thirty-three said. "I love monsters!"

"That would be the usual—and wrong—answer," Ravi said.

Another man raised his hand. Brush-cut, a permanent game face on display, I pegged him as ex-military, one of those macho-tango-delta testosterone freaks in constant need of bungee jumping or battle to stay upright. "Because they're *monsters*," he said. "And it's our sworn duty to show them not to dare mess with humanity!"

Ravi made a game show buzzer sound, indicating the would-be killing machine was wrong. "Also a bad answer," Ravi said. "What about you?"

It took me a few more seconds to realize he was talking to me. "Me?" I asked.

Ravi nodded. "What brings you here today to Monsterland?"

The words were out of my mouth before I could trap them. "I need a job."

Ravi smiled, and his expression chilled me. "Now that's an honest answer—and one that works!"

Filling out applications commenced. Those who'd brought resumes attached them at the back. The form asked for three references. I had one—my brother Vinnie, and he wasn't the most reliable to extol my virtues. But I wasn't sure I wanted them calling him. If he knew I'd applied at Monsterland, it could lead to fresh hell on the home front. I listed him anyway.

Ravi had been correct about the numbers regarding applicants. Only twenty of we hopeful Monsterlanders had stuck around for the next part.

Ravi barely scanned the job applications as they were turned in and said he'd call if interested in the candidate's hire. I handed mine to him and flashed a plastic smile. The red-blooded jarhead and wannabe monster-wrangler stood behind me. We walked out together, but I didn't feel any safer with him guarding my back.

"Remember to stick to the same way you came in," Ravi repeated. "You don't want to get lost before you've even gotten hired, trust me."

By that point, my clothes fit with a damp awkwardness. *Trust him?*

I wouldn't know it for certain until days later, but on that early April afternoon, sweaty and itchy beneath the skin, in my bones, I suspected Ravi Nakur was not to be trusted.

Tunnel to thoroughfare, and from there, back to Gate-F. Sunlight rained down from a cloudless sky the color of comfortable denim, the day deceptively bright. G.I. Jarhead walked close at my six—strength in numbers in case any of the enemy broke through bars, I supposed.

"So much for April showers," I said.

"Huh?"

I snorted a laugh. "Nothing, just making conversation."

He didn't say anything until we were past the gate and striding across the parking lot.

"That prick," he huffed. "He should get so lucky to have someone like Beauregard T. Wolcotte in his unit!"

Luckily, walking a pace ahead of him, my new friend didn't see my face contort with a lunatic's grin. Beauregard? *Bo? G.I. Bo!*

"Yeah, why's that?" I asked in a flat voice.

"Because when the shit gets real, I'm the kind you want ready to whoop monster ass!"

"Okay," I said.

We'd reached my rust bucket. No surprise, parked alongside it was a gigantic black muscle truck, the kind that got half a mile to the gallon on open roads.

"What about you?" he asked.

"What about me?"

G.I. Bo donned a pair of shades intended to make him look cool, intimidating, and undeniably manly. "What's your name?"

I figured this was our first and last conversation. "John Smith," I lied.

"Well, Smith, good luck."

I got in and started the ignition. For a second, I worried that either the engine had chosen that moment to explode or the Great Lakester had revived from the dead and broken out of its glass coffin. But no, it was only the horsepower of G.I. Bo's juggernaut. He waved and peeled off. I sat there for another half-minute, letting my car wake up and wanting some space between me and Beauregard T. Wolcotte. But the Monsterland Hum echoed over my face, so I put the car into drive and rode away.

Two towns over, I pulled along the curb and parked outside my brother Vinnie's Cape-style house. Both Vinnie's and his wife Linda's rides were in the driveway. I'd moved in at the start of winter, which had been miserable enough but made worse by the off-road parking ban from November through April. That was over, thank Christ or Whoever. Not so uplifting was the unspoken sense that my welcome in my brother's house was over as well.

The same sinking weight pressed down on my shoulders and gut as I plodded up the greening lawn and to the front door. Vinnie worked nights—security guard duties at the local hospital—and wouldn't be awake until dinner. Linda dabbled at a lot of different things: pottery, stained glass, and a few shifts a week as a substitute teacher. She wasn't very good at anything she tried, including the teaching, according to my brother and the plethora of junk meant to be art that cluttered their house.

I loosened the top button of my shirt, entered the front door instead of through the kitchen in the hope of avoiding my sister-in-law, and succeeded thanks to my nephew Lonnigan's sharp voice coming from the living room.

"I wanna watch that!"

"And I wanna you to be twenty and not five," Linda countered in a mocking tone.

It was the usual tug of war that took place daily in the house on Brunswick Street. As I snuck down the stairs to my basement accommodations in what had once been the family's rec room—which was a boujee way of calling the space where the old sofa and other hand-me-downs were banished—I wondered which place would haunt my future dreams more: here or Monsterland?

I nestled on the scratchy sofa that was my bed, trying to make sense of it all—the divorce, my situation, a job interview unlike any other. I might have considered that moment the lowest of my life, because nothing seemed certain going forward, and nothing offered hope.

The basement door opened.

"Dinner," Linda called down the stairs in a voice that offered zero welcome. I wasn't hungry, but I was expected. She didn't want me at the table. To not make myself present would lead to other problems. It was a no-win scenario no matter how I responded.

I jumped off the old sofa and plodded up the stairs. The table had been set with disposable plastic plates, paper napkins, and metal cutlery. My older brother sat in his usual chair, his hair a mess of bed-head, his face unshaved, and his eyes droopy from not enough sleep. I noticed Linda had cut her hair, it was still the same dark bob and perpetual expression that looked like she was sucking on a lemon. My nephew kicked his legs against the table.

"Stop that," his mother admonished.

Lonnie didn't.

She set out potato salad from the grocery store deli, peas and carrots in a bowl, and chicken baked in the oven. Silently, we filled our plates. Lonnie protested when his mother spooned peas and carrots onto his. Vinnie ate mostly in silence.

"How did it go today?" my older brother finally asked me.

"I dunno," I answered.

Linda exhaled dismissively through her nostrils. "Did you apply for a job?"

I cut into the chicken. The skin was elastic like latex. The taste wasn't much different. "I had an interview, yeah. Well, sort of an interview."

"Where?" she pressed.

I couldn't tell them. Not her, anyway. Monsterland? I could imagine the blowback from such a revelation—*I won't have you bringing home curses…monsters!…to my house! What about your nephew? Nobody who works there is living here, under this roof!*

"Restaurant," I lied.

"What restaurant?"

"I probably won't get it anyway," I said. "They had a lot of applicants, all of them with more experience than me."

Then my cell vibrated in my back pocket. I sat up, pulled it out, and saw the identity of the caller. My heart attempted to jump out of my ribcage and onto the back of my tongue.

Monsterland.

"I have to take this," I said. I hastened out through the kitchen and to the back patio with its mess of plastic kids toys and old wooden picnic table. I made it to the table but didn't sit. "Hello?"

"I'm calling for Corey Lowen," the familiar and arrogant man's voice said.

"Speaking."

"Corey, this is Ravi Nakur from Monsterland. We've reviewed your application and are very happy to offer you a position as one of our team of Monsterlanders."

I didn't respond until he asked if I was still there. "Yeah, I'm here."

"Did you hear what I said? You have the job."

"Okay."

"You don't sound too excited by the news."

"Stunned, actually."

"Well, get over it. We'd like you to start orientation tomorrow. At eight. We'll have some forms for you to sign. Insurance, liability, those sorts of things. The necessary evils of working around real monsters."

He laughed at this. I automatically chuckled, too.

"You'll need to wear khakis and sneakers. We'll provide you with the uniform shirts—"

I recalled the black polo tops with the cartoon vampire bat.

"—and be sure to enter the park through the same gate. Gate—"

"F'ed," I said.

I pulled my car into the lot and sat there with the front windows rolled down. Warm spring air fragrant with the sweet smell of the surrounding pines wafted in. The voice in my head told me to turn around, drive back…But to what? Certainly not home. The house on Brunswick Street was a way station, a holding pattern. Worse, Limbo—land of lost souls.

I hadn't slept for more than a few hours the night before and imagined I looked haggard like my brother. A glance in the rearview mirror confirmed it.

You'll need a physical, Ravi said in my thoughts. *To confirm you're capable of the job's demands.*

I don't have a doctor, I'd told him. No insurance, no primary care physician.

There'd been a slight pause. *No problem, we'll have our doctor on staff clear you for work.*

Their doctor? I wondered just how desperate for new hires Monsterland was that they were so eager to cut corners.

I rolled up the windows and got out. The Monsterland Hum was back, this time chilly and electric beneath the cheeks of my butt. It reminded me of that invisible cold you experience after jolting awake from a nightmare. I adjusted the seat of my pants en route to the gate. It didn't help.

The same chubby girl with glasses and dark hair who'd walked all of us potential Monsterlanders to the conference room guarded Gate-F. "Good morning," she chirped way too brightly at so early an hour.

"Morning. My name's Corey Lowen—first day on the job."

She checked a clipboard with a printout and waved me through. "You are good to go. Someone will direct you to Human Resources once you're on the main thoroughfare."

I thanked her and wandered in. The little acid voice in my mind taunted me with the reminder that it was now too late to turn back. I'd stepped through the entrance and there'd be no exit from Monsterland. I was trapped.

On the thoroughfare, it struck me how non-threatening my surroundings appeared on the surface. In the glow of morning sunshine, I could have been standing in any amusement park or beachside tourist trap, not a destination where genuine creatures of the night and legend were housed in captivity. The air maintained its piney sweetness. The sound of voices and a woman's laugh filtered in from somewhere out of my purview. No one waited to greet me on the path of sun-blasted asphalt, as I'd been promised, and the temptation to wander, to explore on my own, possessed me. I tipped a glance toward the back of the mummy exhibit. The exterior wall was painted a dusty gray. But the front was a whole different animal. From my angle, I could see the details of one of the three pyramids and the replica of the Sphinx that guarded the entrance—along with, no doubt, more than a few curse protections and wards meant to overpower the residents inside who were still under the influence of Ancient Egypt.

"Smith," a man's voice addressed me from behind.

I only turned because of the sudden sound, not because I believed the comment was meant for me. Then I remembered the lie I'd told the man who strutted up to me, confidence broadcast by his spare smile, his eyes hidden behind those expensive shades. Beauregard T. Wolcotte extended his gigantic hand for a shake. I accepted, because that's what men do when offered such a gesture.

"You made it," he said.

G.I. Bo's hand squeezed down on mine with enough strength to snap the bones of lesser men. I responded with as much as I had and waited for the shake to end, finally saying, "You too."

"Of course they hired me," he said and released my smarting fingers and palm. "Would have been a mistake on their part to let *this* go." He folded his arms. I noticed the ink running down one's underside: a sword and a link of chain wrapped around the other's upper bicep, just poking out of the short sleeve of his shirt.

"My name's not John Smith," I said.

"Oh?"

"It's Corey—Corey Lowen."

G.I. Bo didn't comment but instead seemed to take it in silently, processing this bit of intelligence in a military fashion.

"Figured you should know, we being fellow Monsterlanders and all."

G.I. Bo uncrossed his arms and extended his same shake hand and, for a terrible second, I worried that he wanted us to repeat the greeting. To my relief, I saw he'd made a fist, the knuckles aimed my way. "Brother Monsterlanders," he said.

"Welcome to the Brotherhood," I answered lightly, knocked knuckles, and then, not sure why, followed up by miming an explosion.

"Gentleman," another voice interrupted, a woman's.

We turned toward her. Mid-twenties, I guessed, her mane of dark hair wrangled into a ponytail, athletic body displayed in jeans and Monsterland black polo shirt, radio clipped to belt. Even her crooked smile was beautiful. Though of that latter detail, I noticed a kind of heaviness trying to weigh down her lips. It was the same gravity that sat on my shoulders, a force born of life's hardships. I recognized that in her and wondered what she'd been through to earn her battle scars.

"I'm not sure about my new pal Smith here," G.I. Bo said. "About him being a gentleman." He laughed at his own joke.

She answered with a raised eyebrow and a wider smile. "I'm Martine from Human Resources, if you'll come with me."

Bo gave my shoulder a playful smack and I unconsciously winced as we followed Martine farther along the thoroughfare, past the door to the tunnel, and deeper into the park.

"The Hum?" I asked.

"What about it?"

"It's different from yesterday," I said, leaving out the part about how it had crept down the seat of my pants and was playing hide-and-seek between my butt cheeks. "Stronger."

"You'll get used to it. After a week, you won't even feel it anymore," Martine said.

"Good, because its got me by the—" G.I. Bo started only to stop, the sentence left unfinished.

"Yes?" Martine prodded. "It's got you by what?"

Bo removed his shades. I saw what had him suddenly so mute.

"*Nuts,*" I gasped.

We had just reached an open plaza between exhibits, rides, concession stands, and buildings. Rising above all of it was a large domed structure whose roof kept out the direct sun. A series of lights recessed in the dome's ceiling illuminated the massive fish tank structure beneath.

In the murk of that nightmare aquarium, the corpse of the Great Lakes Monster was entombed. It was displayed on its spine. The sheer and hideous awesomeness of the dead giant made breathing almost impossible. Blinking, too. Even at a distance, we could see the details of the monster's head, turned in our direction. Worse, its eyes; they were opened and staring blankly our way. The Great Lakester had also lost the ability to blink and seemed to study us with rage and malevolent intent.

Bo swore. That helped me to thaw enough to suck down a sip of air and also to blink.

"Like I said," Martine sighed, "after a while, you get used to it. This way."

Her words haunted me past the front door of a little bungalow located in a corner of the park that was backed against the outer brick wall. *Get used to any of this?* To get used to the wide eyes of the leviathan that had come striding out of Lake Erie on a rainy summer day without warning and still without explanation? Or any of the other horrors that were housed around us? The sasquatches made as commonplace as gorillas in other zoos? The quintet of vampires or trio of mummies? The ancient dinosaur-thing swimming in circles in its enclosed bathtub like killer whales in aquariums?

The small coffee and buck menu biscuit I'd wolfed down before arriving at Monsterland did back flips in my belly. A sour burp clawed its way up my throat.

"There are theories, of course," Martine continued, her voice couched in a white noise whine that could have been more Monsterland Hum or only simple disbelief within the overwhelmed gray matter inside my skull. "That it was a military experiment gone amuck or something created by all the toxic waste dumped into the Great Lakes over the decades. There's even one school of belief that it came down on a meteorite and grew after hatching, but nothing's been proven. The Great Lakester might end up being a mystery that's never solved."

For a room set in a monster-themed park with real monsters, Human Resources was a bit of a letdown. The outer office contained four chairs identical to the torture devices from yesterday and the conference room, work safety posters—none of which bore any likenesses of monsters—and various framed policy printouts. Boring stuff. Past the front desk, presently manned by the same chubby woman with glasses and dark hair, was another conference room where three more new hires waited. I recognized them all from the job fair.

"Wassup, bros and sisters," Bo said, his cockiness back and on full display.

One nerdy guy in glasses offered up a high-five. I winced even before G.I. Bo connected with the kind of swing that would have launched a baseball out and over the park. The kid recoiled. I figured holding his pen after that was quite the miserable task.

Bo took one of the empty seats, at first oblivious to the forms waiting on the desk in front of him. I sat and scanned mine. *Liability*, I noted. *Insurance.*

"So, when do we start feeding the vampires and wrestling with Bigfoot?" Bo asked, bookending the question with a smug laugh.

"You don't," Martine said, real cool. "Not for a long time. Not until you've been properly trained. Wouldn't want the vampires eating *you*, would we?"

"I don't know," Bo countered. "That Ursula's not bad on the eyes. And I dig her go-go boots." He raised his big hand again for a high-five. This time, the nerd shrank away.

"Baroness Ursula von Ullmer is not to be underestimated," Martine said, all humor gone from her expression. "Do you know how many lives she's taken since the late 1800s?"

The nerd raised his damaged hand. "It's been confirmed that Baroness Ullmer is responsible for one hundred and sixty-four deaths and subsequent transformations that we know of, but it's estimated she could be responsible for three times that number."

Martine pinned Bo with a serious, unblinking stare. Bo's arrogance deflated, more so as a result of her gaze than the nerd's reality check. Silence briefly hung over the entire conference room. "You'll need to fill out all of the forms in front of you. Anyone who hasn't yet been cleared by a physical within the past six months will need to see our doctor today in order to start the next phase of orientation."

"Lemme guess—Doctor Frankenstein?" Bo joked.

The nerd chuckled. Other new Monsterlanders cast disapproving looks.

"Actually, our Doctor Wandry has never reanimated corpses to my knowledge," Martine said. "Mister Wolcotte, is the comedy routine done?"

"Huh?"

"Because monsters are serious business, and here at Monsterland, we take that business seriously."

Her smackdown was effective, so much so that G.I. Bo didn't crack another joke throughout the rest of the orientation. Enough that I kind of pitied him. It was like he got emasculated in that one verbal bitch-slap.

And then it was over and on to that business of monsters.

Four of us went to see Doctor Ivy Wandry at what passed for Monsterland's First Aid Station—me, G.I. Bo, the nerd, whose name was Curtis Nesbitt the Third, and Carla Gerritt, an older woman who looked fairly capable of wrestling sasquatches by the tribe.

Like Human Resources, the First Aid Station could have existed anywhere banal in the modern world. Nothing monstrous identified it as being part of the theme park devoted to monsters except for the cartoon vampire bat on the black polo shirt worn by the receptionist. We four waited. Curtis Nesbitt the Third was shown in first. G.I. Bo sat on one side of me, the lady wrestler the other. The floor vibrated—though not from the Monsterland Hum but Bo's nervous tick. His right leg bounced up and down in an agitated—and agitating—cadence.

"Hey, ants-in-the-pants," Carla Gerritt snapped.

Bo stilled his jimmy-leg dance and shot her a scowl.

Carla settled back and pulled a magazine from her tote. Bo flashed a look meant to appear cool and in control, but that only made me pity him more.

"So, dude, what do you think about all this?" Bo asked me.

I shrugged. "I'm not sure."

"You got a girlfriend? What does she think?"

Not sure why, I came clean. "Divorced. Recently. Ink's barely dry on the papers."

"Oh," he said.

"What do you think?" I asked despite knowing the answer.

Bo's smug grin snuck back. "Me? I can't wait to get out there. This is like a calling to me! It's us against them, *yeah!*"

"What does your girlfriend think?"

Bo's confidence evaporated. "Not seeing anyone at the present. But I get dates, sure—plenty of them."

Carla eyed us over the top of her glossy magazine, which was devoted to the subject of sewing.

"I do!" Bo snapped.

Carla cleared her throat. The minutes dragged onward. About half an hour later, Curtis Nesbitt the Third emerged from the exam room looking no worse than when he'd entered.

"Mister Lowen, Doctor Wandry will see you now," the receptionist announced.

I stood. Bo offered me a high-five. I declined and wandered into the room.

It was your typical doctor's office—boxes containing small, medium, and large disposable gloves lined up in a clear plastic holder on one wall, two chairs, a sink, cabinets and drawers, and an examination table within reach of gadgets on another wall designed for poking into ears and checking out eyes.

I sat in one of the chairs and waited, aware of the silent echo of the Hum and how it sat in my belly. The antiseptic air vibrated. I recalled the terrifying image of the Great Lakester and remembered that since, plenty of the government's resources and attention had gone to the region. There were observation posts along all the shores of the Great Lakes and plenty beneath the water, both staffed and remotely operated. Every water molecule contained within the lakes had been sifted and studied. Satellites in geosynchronous orbit kept watch for a repeat of the nightmarish event.

That monster was *here*.

A familiar, dragging unhappiness embraced me. I thought of Vinnie, Linda, Lonnigan, and the house on Brunswick Street. The sudden urge to walk out of the room, the First Aid Station, the park, get in my car, and drive, just drive, tempted me. But the weight held me immobilized and I had little more than a quarter of a tank of gas in my old heap.

A polite knock sounded on the other side of the door. I bid my visitor to enter. In breezed a woman dressed in pale blue hospital scrubs and sparkly sneakers. Her black hair was pulled back into a casual ponytail. Her glasses matched her sneakers. "Mister Lowen?" she greeted.

At first, I was so taken aback by her youthful exuberance that I didn't respond. Then, clearing my throat, I said lightly, "Mister Lowen was my dad. Now that's my brother Vinnie."

"Okay. Corey?"

"Present," I said like some class clown in high school and then felt stupid for the quip. Stupider.

She set down my chart beside the sink and reached for a pair of gloves—medium. "I'm Doctor Wandry. Nice to meet you."

"Likewise," I said.

"How about you have a seat over here?" She adjusted the exam table, flipping its back up and into a bench.

I scooted over and sat. My legs dangled like Lonnie's at the dinner table.

Doctor Wandry picked up the clipboard with chart. "First, let's start with meds."

"Meds?"

"Are you on any prescriptions?"

"No."

"Drugs? Do you use anything illicit?"

"No."

"Not even marijuana?"

"No."

She jotted a note on the chart. "Good, because you will be required to submit to random drug screenings, starting now." Doctor Wandry pulled a plastic urine cup out of one of the drawers and set it on the counter.

She ran through a list of afflictions and asked about family histories—cancer, heart disease, diabetes, and mental illness. I thought about telling her what had happened with my father that Saturday morning in my youth; how, after, he distanced himself from me, grew to hate me. But I didn't.

"No, none of that," I lied.

"How much alcohol do you consume daily?"

I laughed. She eyed me from the corner of her glasses. Like with G.I. Bo, I came clean. "I'm divorced. The ex. She had a drinking problem. I haven't touched a drop in…oh, six months? Besides, even the cheap stuff is too expensive for me right now. I live on a lumpy old sofa that smells like wet dog in my brother's basement."

"Your brother Vinnie, right?" she asked.

I realized I'd blathered too much and suffered a rush of red embarrassment. "Yeah, Vinnie."

She pulled a stethoscope from one of the drawers. "I'm going to listen to your heart and lungs now."

I sucked down deep breaths while she checked out my airbags. She pressed the metal disc over my heart. Up close, she smelled faintly of floral perfume, something light and pleasant. Something *happy*, like her sparkly sneakers and eyeglass frames.

"Everything sounds perfect," she said.

"What a relief—*I'm alive!*"

She flashed a smile while jotting more notes on my chart. "Around here, you have to make sure."

"I can see why."

"You're in great health, Mister Lowen. *Corey.*"

"Thanks."

"What do you think of all this?"

It was presented casually, like simple conversation—the weather or sports. But I sensed more to the question.

"We walked past the giant aquarium containing the body of the Great Lakes Monster," I said. "And I wanted to run away, to hide under the nearest bed."

"Honest," she remarked almost to herself.

"Yeah, I have that problem lately. Except when it comes to telling my family about this job."

She smiled again. "The last protesters abandoned their signs outside the gates five, six years ago. But we still get some nut inside the park that wants to free the thing from Loch Ness or, heaven forbid, the quintet of vampires. Because its inhumane to want to profit from their captivity. Do you think it's inhumane?"

Something warned me that the actual interview hadn't ended. I was still being tested. "Inhumane? They're safe here, right? Which means all the people who they could potentially hurt or worse out there in the world are safe, too."

She ceased writing. "Agreed. A pleasure meeting you, Corey. Welcome to the Monsterland Family."

I thanked her, stood, and returned to the waiting room. They called in Bo next. Even before the door was closed behind him, he'd stripped out of his shirt, revealing an obscenely buff and hairless torso and washboard abs, the American flag inked onto his right upper pectorals.

"You can keep your shirt on," the receptionist said.

Bo snorted a laugh. "No, *you* can keep your shirt on, sweet thing."

The receptionist stiffened. "Seriously, Mister Wolcotte, put your shirt back on."

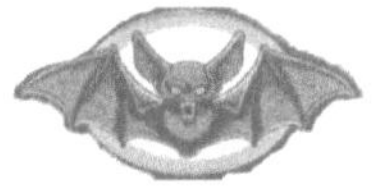

About an hour later, Martine collected us and we returned to Human Resources. There, we were given our two changes of Monsterland black polo shirts, shown the break room with its vending machines and coffee maker, our individual lockers, and the time clock. Orientation and training were paid for, she reminded us. I'd earned my first two hours and could afford takeout at one of your more common franchise drive throughs if I stuck to the dollar menu.

"Now, it's important that you get the lay of the land," Martine said.

Bo snickered. Martine ignored him.

"Expect to do a fair amount of walking and to be constantly on your feet. Comfortable sneakers are a must, in fact, it's wise to keep a second pair in your locker. You'll understand why after we take the official tour."

A look of mischief glinted in her gaze.

"You ready to see Monsterland?"

Sunlight streamed down as the balmy spring breeze attempted to deceive me. We passed games where visitors could pitch three basketballs at a hoop for the chance to win a stuffed sasquatch with big feet and a dopey, harmless smile or a neon green stuffed plesiosaurus—lacking carnivore teeth, of course.

There was the Transylvanian Café, where one could enjoy the park's famed grilled Monster Cheese Sandwich or iced coffee or cookies in the shapes of vampire bats, mummies, Jack-o'lanterns, and werewolves. Past that, Martine showed us the merry-go-round. All of the steeds were black with menacing red eyes that lit up when the ride was in motion like escapees from the old British Hammer Horror films. Among them prowled kelpies, loping werewolves, and goblins. Rising behind that was the Ferris wheel or, in this case, the Monsterland Fear-is Wheel. Over all towered the tracks and loops of the Dragon Express.

Nothing ran at that early hour, but the throng of visitors would soon be heard after the gates opened at noon.

"That's all the easy stuff," Martine said. "Now, how about I show you the real heart of Monsterland? After the tour, you'll all be expected to sit for a Monsterland ID badge, which you're required to wear at all times upon entering the park," Martine explained. "Not only for the purpose of identifying you but as a safeguard."

"Safeguard?" Carla parroted.

We had neared the mummy exhibit. Ancient Egypt rose above us thanks to a trio of three-story interconnected pyramids and a sphinx twice the size of an elephant. Using her ID badge to open the doors of the central pyramid, Martine led us through to a foyer decorated in exquisitely detailed replicas of Egyptian statuary and stone walls covered in carved hieroglyphs. The air was cool and smelled faintly of popcorn and bubble gum—the leftover proof of the previous day's foot traffic, I supposed, bottled up inside the somber tomb. A pair of lights hung down from the ceiling, one green, the other red. The green one was lit. Behind those lights rose a tall, thick glass window, the other side dark. The air vibrated with the Hum, and that echo grew more distinct as we neared the glass.

"You'll notice those two lights. Pray the green one's always lit. It means the exhibit—more so, the exhibit's residents—are secure. In case you find it red, inside each of the monster enclosures is a lockbox," Martine instructed. "Should you ever get trapped on the wrong side of the barrier under Condition Red in any of our exhibits, you can open the lockbox with your ID. Inside is a safeguard specific to the monster housed there—a spray can filled with concentrated silver and garlic in the vampire exhibit—"

"Are you for real?" G.I. Bo interrupted.

Martine's mouth tightened. "A flamethrower in Frankenstein's Castle—Frelling's monster doesn't care for fire."

"What's in the sasquatch lockup—a bar of soap?" Bo said and then cracked up at his own joke.

Martine blinked. "Mister Wolcotte, are you listening to anything I'm saying?" Bo started to answer. "Because," Martine continued, cutting him off before he could speak, "the information I'm attempting to relay could save your life or that of one of your coworkers."

Bo's face turned red. Martine shot a look at him. Bo broke focus and Martine won the staring contest. She lifted the radio from her belt. "Monroe, can you light things up?"

"Roger that," a man's voice crackled over the squawk box.

The other side of the glass lit with a blinding, white intensity. The source of that glow came from a false sun—an incandescent bulb network over a stage crafted to resemble a desert scene. A mural of the pyramids decorated the farthest wall. Several life-like palms stood at intervals. Sun-bleached sand provided a foundation for the six gold- and jewel-encrusted sarcophagi propped upright and open, three on either side of a stone pillar decorated in hieroglyphs rising up from the middle of the exhibit.

"We have three mummies in the protected enclosure," Martine said. "You're looking at the Pharaoh Rahm."

And there it was, something that should have been unthinkable outside the realm of the cinema and various creature features. The hunched, emaciated figure wrapped in desiccated muslin rags plodded halfway from one sarcophagus on the right side of the exhibit to an empty coffin on the left. Its steps were dragging and slow, affording us time to study it. The figure more resembled a child than a hulking menace and couldn't have been more than four feet tall.

"It's a kid," Bo chuckled.

Curtis Nesbitt the Third said, "Actually, Rahm the Omnipotent was thirteen when he was poisoned by a jealous successor. And the Egyptians of the time were physically much smaller than Homo sapiens of today."

Nerd, I thought, just as a chill tickled me unpleasantly somewhere close to my rectum.

I watched, not speaking, while Rahm the Omnipotent lumbered on. Long seconds later, he reached the empty sarcophagus and curled into its shadowy confines. As soon as he did, another mummy appeared from one of the three coffins on that side of the display and, like Rahm, proceeded toward the right-hand area. Not lost on me was how the mummy, whose bandages were a robin's egg blue color, seemed to jolt out of the sarcophagus.

"The tombs are wired with electricity," Martine said as though reading my thoughts. "Otherwise, they'd just lie in there, which gets pretty boring real fast. For that kind of mummy, you can go to any metropolitan museum."

"So you give them a little zap and *voilà*, mummies on the move," I said.

"They're here to be noticed," she said.

"Who's that one? And why is it blue?" asked Carla.

"That's Bezteht," Martine answered. "And the color's called Egyptian Blue—it's the result of the first human-made dye."

"Calcium copper silicate," the nerd said. "It was meant to mimic lapis lazuli, a semi-precious stone thought to have mystical properties."

"Jeeze, it's like being in science class," Bo said.

"Listen up, Mister Wolcotte, you might learn something."

Bezteht completed her journey to the sarcophagus vacated by Rahm. After half a minute, the third mummy emerged. This one was taller than the other two, its condition not as precise. The emaciated remains of its face peeked through gaps in its rotted bandages. It gazed at us through empty sockets, and the chill beneath my backside worsened. I saw Carla shudder. Even Bo held his tongue.

"Who's he?" Curtis asked.

"Him? Now that is a very good question, and one we can't answer. That mummy has never been identified," Martine said. "It's a mystery. We call him Stray."

She pointed out the emergency lockbox bolted behind one of the palm trees and mostly out of view from the public side of the window.

"What's in there to ward off mummies?" asked Curtis.

"Let's hope you're never in the position to find out," Martine said.

The mysterious third mummy completed its toil to reach the other side of the exhibit. No sooner had it crawled into the empty sarcophagus then Rahm got zapped again and was on his move across the sands. It struck me how terrible the reality on the other side of the glass truly was. Though long dead, the trio of cursed souls was constantly denied rest in order to perform for Monsterland's paying public. I hadn't been particularly sympathetic to mummies in general before entering the exhibit, but on the way out, I found myself feeling sorry for their fate.

"Don't touch the bars," Martine warned.

"It ain't the bars," Bo chuckled and waved a hand in front of his nose.

The stench hit us well before we reached the oasis of dense trees and shrubbery wreathed in a cage with crisscrossed branches growing and winding within the bars to about thirty feet high on all sides but the observation area. The overhead gridwork made escape by scurrying up impossible. My imagination translated the funk into locker rooms and the insides of a dirty laundry hamper times a hundred.

Like much of the park's safeguards, the bars to the sasquatch enclosure had been electrified, according to the signs for caution that ringed it. What we approached was, I realized, not much different than any monkey house in a zoo. Only here, the primates were beyond rare. They were the stuff of legend.

"I don't see—?" started Carla.

"That's why they were able to stay hidden for so long. A kind of natural camouflage—or *super*natural. We're not entirely sure which." Martine again raised her radio. "Yeah, Monroe, if you'd be so kind to light 'er up."

"Roger that, Martine," the voice at the other end of the line said.

I felt more than heard the *pop*, which rippled through the air and traveled past skin and even bone to a place that could have been soul. From my fellow new Monsterlanders, the chorus of gasps and swears uttered beneath breaths indicated they'd felt it as well. Beyond the bars, the effect was even more pronounced.

Shrubs shook and swept aside. Ominous, hulking figures that hadn't been obvious to the eye before now were, seeming to have stepped directly out of the trunks of trees. I made out four distinct shapes that grew clearer the longer I stared.

"It's kind of like a cattle prod," Martine said, though her voice sounded a lot farther away than the actual few yards. "Sonic-based, it shorts out their ability to camouflage for three minutes and change."

"The usual amount of time for an average solar eclipse," said Curtis. "Curious."

"I'm starting to wonder about you," said Bo. "If you're *curious.*"

Carla tsked. I expected Martine to lay into G.I. Bo, but at that moment, my concentration was on the enclosure where the four residents had become fully tangible. All four leered at us with wide, unblinking stares. The whites around those dark pupils glowed. I heard a low, throaty growl magnified by four distinct voices that merged together, becoming a kind of guttural chant reminiscent of Buddhist monks. Only this one lacked any hypnotic quality and conjured gooseflesh across my bare arms.

That growl was a warning, and I knew without being told that had those electrified bars not been there, we'd all be dead.

"The one with the scar on her cheek is Big Momma," Martine said. "We're not sure how she got that beauty mark— grizzly bear, maybe. But not even the boldest grizzly bear would be that brave. The small guy over there—"

The "small guy" stood, I guessed, at well over seven feet tall.

"—that's Junior. He's either younger or the beta to the other two males. Meet Big Daddy and Uncle Lou."

The remaining specimens towered close to eight. Their forearms were masses of fur and muscle. The knot in my gut that I'd arrived with to the park was back, only now grown worse. The thick and musky stink burned in my next sip of air. As I stared at Uncle Lou, who leered back at me with the clearest hatred, the stupidest thought crossed my mind: What if my clothes picked up that rank odor and I brought it back with me to the house that wasn't a home?

I blinked ... and Uncle Lou was gone along with Junior, Big Momma, and Big Daddy.

"Three minutes and change," Martine said. "Just like a solar eclipse." She asked us if we wanted to see them again and held up the walky-talky, ready to have Monroe zap the enclosure a second time.

"I'm good," I said.

Bo shifted in place. "Yeah, I could use some fresh air."

We moved on.

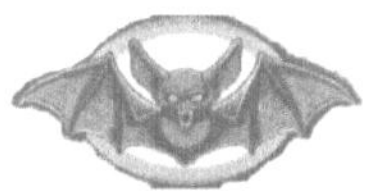

Like the sasquatch enclosure, we smelled the loch before we saw it. The giant aquarium was housed in a structure that resembled the exterior of a hockey rink on the outside, but one that had been dressed up like a movie set. Animatronic dinosaurs stood guard outside where a sign implored park visitors to:

See the Monster From Prehistoric Times!

As I suspected, the long-necked, robot brachiosaurus swung around at us as we passed into the hockey rink and the allosaurus let forth with a nightmare roar.

Like I said, we could smell the loch…or the *lake* recreated inside the building. The chemically treated water lent a somber note of dampness to the surrounding atmosphere.

Again using her ID badge, Martine passed us through the main entrance and inside the structure that housed the creature captured in Loch Ness and re-housed here in Monsterland. Signs in the lobby told of the tale—the special cage into which Nestor had been lured; the history of the carnivorous species, of which ninety-one fossils and skeletons and one living specimen had been discovered. Historical images graced the walls. The cool humidity grew even more pronounced.

Beyond the lobby doors, stairs soared up to a viewing platform and down to another level, this lower recess set before a glass wall. We headed down. The water beyond the reinforced window swirled, the current murky and green-tinged. Somewhere inside that soup was Nestor, the monster from Loch Ness.

"Technically, the creature isn't a monster but a survivor from an early epoch," the nerd said. "Like the Komodo dragon, crocodiles, and the coelacanth—the dinosaur fish found off the coast of Madagascar."

"Whatever," Bo sighed. "It's here in a cage. That makes it a monster."

I stepped closer to the glass. Somewhere on the observation deck above was a lockbox containing the means for survival if we somehow got trapped with Nestor and our lives were placed in jeopardy. I wondered what the lockbox contained—a fresh fish to toss at Nestor's open jaws and all those sharp teeth?

A shadow stirred in the murk. Faster than should have been possible, it charged out of the background and at the glass. A loud *whoosh* shook the aquarium tank. Expecting the surge less than I had, Bo let out a high-pitched, girlish scream and jumped back on instinct. The only one of us who didn't flinch was Martine.

"Someone's hungry," Martine said.

Nestor measured eleven feet from head to tail, but in our horror was many times that—even bigger than the Great Lakester. It swept around the tank after throwing itself at the sturdy glass and us, circled its enclosure, and made another pass. This time, I got a clearer look at it—the four lower fins, the long neck, the head, jaws, and all those sharp teeth.

We continued to the next attraction—Frankenstein's Castle. Technically, the thing around which the exhibit had been built was *Frelling's* monster. Inspired by the notion of Mary Shelley's novel and, more so, a plethora of movies, Galabraith

Frelling, "the maddest scientist who ever lived," set to work on reanimating stitched-together body parts into the abomination discovered inside his Geneva laboratory. Geneva, New York, not Switzerland.

Martine unlocked the castle gates, and we entered. Again, no lack of detail had been paid to the theatrical setting. Long tapestries covered the walls. Gothic oil paintings of Mary Wollenstone Shelley, Boris Karloff as The Monster, and Frelling himself were hung around the lobby for effect along with cinema posters in frames. Beyond the open doors, a cleaning crew was in the process of washing walls and floors. The industrial cleaner barely covered up a pungent, antiseptic note. The light over their heads was green.

The main exhibit was in the shape of an amphitheater that circled three-quarters of an open stage. Rising at the sides of the stage were a pair of dormant electrical conductors—*de rigueur* for any mad scientist's lair. I guessed they'd be in full crackle mode once the park opened for visitors. The rest of the stage had been designed to theme—one wall devoted to shelves of beakers filled with colorful liquids and racks of test tubes. At the opposite side was a cot and seated upon it, chained at both ankles, was an inelegant hominid figure clad only in black pajama pants whose torso, throat, and wrists showed plenty of scar tissue.

"Oh my God," Curtis gasped beside me. "It's him—the Frelling Monster!"

The creature looked over at us. One of its eyes was larger than the other, too big in its socket for it to blink. The other considered us not so much with hatred as I'd seen in some of the other monster exhibits but a kind of melancholy. I stared into its one functioning eye and pitied the monster, imagining its expression like that of any other unhappy caged animal in a zoo. Its gaze seemed to tell me that it had given up and was only breathing because its lungs still worked.

"Frelling's Creation, the man without a soul," Martine said.

Not sure why, I said, "How do you know?"

"Know what?"

"That it doesn't have a soul? I mean, by what authority does *anyone* have to make such a claim? It's not like you can do a test to find out who has a soul and who doesn't."

I hadn't planned for my voice to rise to that level, but it did. Only after the words were past my lips did I hear them echo off the glass beakers and test tubes. A clanking of chains followed. I looked down the aisles to see Frelling's Monster stand and shuffle closer toward us.

"Easy, guy," G.I. Bo said. He clapped me on the shoulder with enough force that it stung. "You're upsetting the monster."

I stepped away from Bo. On stage, the creature born from spare parts was looking at me through its one good eye and had raised its right arm. I noted the long, dirty fingernails as it beckoned to me with a wave. My insides cramped. A chill teased the fine hairs at the nape of my neck. I fought it, failed. The shiver tumbled down my backbone, curiously hotter than icy.

"We know," Martine said, "because Galabraith Frelling butchered seven men to make that one creature."

"Isn't he entitled to the same human rights as the rest of us?" This came from Curtis Nesbitt the Third.

"Spare parts don't have rights," Martine said calmly. "An amputated hand from a murdered body isn't owed anything."

I thought her statement was cold yet also practiced. Clearly, she'd answered such charges before enough times to know all the correct responses.

Grunting, the Frelling Monster withdrew the offer of its right-less hand and plodded back to its humble bed, where it slumped down and pulled into a fetal curl atop the threadbare covers. My sympathy toward the creature doubled. An unpleasant warmth lay over my skin.

"What happened to him wasn't *his* fault," I grumbled while cleaning crews continued to clean. I fell under the unwanted scrutiny of my fellow new hires.

"You heard the lady, Smith," Bo said. "Ol' Frankie here doesn't have a soul." He laughed, which I hated, and again smacked me on the back, this time with both of his mitts, which I hated more.

We moved toward the exit. A dark emotion pursued me like an unwanted second shadow back into the daylight and fresh air.

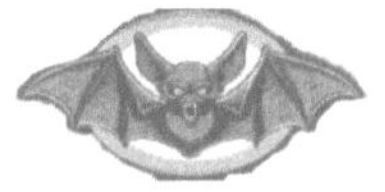

"What do they do when the sun's still out?" Carla asked.

"They sleep."

We passed a pair of Monsterland security guards, a duo Bo would have fit perfectly among, and entered the vampire exhibit. I figured a couple of ex-military muscle goons were more for unwanted guests trying to get into the place than those inside breaking out. From what I'd gathered, the baroness and her four underlings could rip off a person's head within the fraction of a second it took you to blink, which was why their capture was legendary.

Of course, the exterior of the vampire exhibit was designed to resemble a haunted house. It was more Hollywood set design. Inside was a different story. Along the ceilings ran numerous pipes filled with, we learned, a corrosive solution of silver and garlic. At any second that cocktail, deadly to vampires, could be unleashed upon the entire enclosure. Signs posted at intervals warned to not stare into any vampire's gaze and for friends and family members to be vigilant for signs that loved ones were in the process of being glamoured.

"Luckily, that hasn't happened too often," Martine said. "We like to stay ahead of beguilings."

We passed through two more sets of security guards and doors before reaching the actual enclosure. Like others we'd encountered on that morning's tour, the vampire exhibit was sealed behind thick, reinforced glass.

"Two-way mirror," Martine said. "We can see in, but they can't see out. On their side, it's just mirror and, as you might recall, vampires aren't able to cast a reflection, so they generally avoid looking at the glass, which is yet another safety measure."

Beyond our side of the barrier spread a glimpse into another time. Shag carpeting and oil on velvet paintings decorated the large space along with minimalist furniture—chairs that looked even more uncomfortable on the human ass than those in the theme park's training rooms. An old phonograph housed in a mahogany cabinet stood in one corner with its top raised and records in sleeves displayed. Another side of the room boasted a wet bar. All of it looked very Swinging Singles—a snapshot from an earlier era. And quite, quite, tacky.

Five singles swung from the ceiling upside down like bats in a cave. The members of Baroness Ursula von Ullmer's coven hung onto the ceiling by their bare feet. From what I could see of their bodies, which rested mostly in shadows, they were all dressed otherwise impeccably—two women in formfitting cat suits, three men in Nehru jackets and trousers. All slept with their arms crossed over their chests in funereal poses.

"Far out," mumbled Bo. "They almost look like a fun time."

"You've got an unusual definition of fun," quipped Curtis.

Bo scowled. "I'm fun!"

"I meant," Curtis said, aiming a finger at the quintet of upside down corpses suspended above the hip pad from another time, "that's no dance party that any of us wants to be invited to!"

Martine said nothing. We stared in for another few seconds, then the view shifted from fascinating to mundane.

"Don't you, I dunno…*zap* them or anything?" asked Carla. "Like the mummies and those hairy ape things in the big cage?"

"No, we let them sleep," said Martine. "It's best not to stir them into a wild panic."

I glanced back up. The baroness's eyes were open and aimed down at us, at *me*. I jolted.

Bo came up behind me and clamped both hands on my shoulders. "Someone's hot for you, Smith," he chuckled.

The baroness's eyes closed shut. I shook off the unpleasant rush of heat and stepped out of Bo's touch. "I told you, my name's not Smith!"

Martine nodded to the security guards, and we moved on.

There were gift shops that sold Monsterland t-shirts, mugs, glasses, and stuffed monsters; bumper cars whose posts snapped and crackled with electricity and released the stink of burnt ozone into the air; and the park's version of a caterpillar. Stands sold cotton candy, smash burgers and fries, slushies, and deep-fried treats.

We circled back along the walking trails that meandered through those otherwise mundane features to the last attraction, which was anything but.

The giant fish tank that contained the body of the Great Lakester.

We fell beneath its unblinking death-stare. The day's warmth evaporated. The Hum was back at upped intensity, stroking me in unpleasant ripples.

"And our friend here needs no introduction," said Martine. "You all remember him."

"Or *her*," said Curtis. "There's some speculation that the lake monster was female."

Martine smiled, though the gesture was one of tolerance, not actual happiness. "There is that. But what's important to remember is that what you're looking at is a testament—to both great tragedy and human triumph. The monster claimed upwards of a thousand lives before it was taken down. As far as we know, it's the first and last of its kind on the planet. And it's the exhibit that draws the greatest crowds, even though it's dead."

I worked my gaze up to the giant's head and those terrible eyes. Winter slithered over my flesh. At any second, I expected the monster to twitch, to wake up, to crash through the reinforced glass as it had so many of Cleveland's concrete and steel structures, and to grab at us. Grab me.

"Any questions?" Martine asked.

I had so many. Too many. But none would make their way past my paralyzed lips.

"Okay, then, if you're ready, it's time for your training to begin."

Curtis Nesbitt the Third and I got assigned shadowing duties at the front gate. I couldn't have felt less relevant as I watched a girl who couldn't have been older than eighteen scan tickets and phones and wrap bracelets around the wrists of visitors who streamed to the park in hundreds, perhaps thousands. Those bracelets identified the wearer as having paid for one of three plans—the Monsterland Basic, which got them through the gate; the Silver, which included rides; and the Gold, which covered rides and access into the monster exhibits. I suppose it could have been worse. Carla was sent to one of the concession stands, G.I. Bo to the gift shop.

"Gold really is the bargain," the girl, whose name was Edie, said. "I mean, what's the point of visiting Monsterland if you don't see the monsters? The cheapos end up paying at each exhibit anyway."

The afternoon wore on and my body forgot that it was in its late-twenties. Aches rippled up my calves and sang from my lower back. All the standing and walking reminded me I'd aged since the divorce. At three, Martine returned to the front gate to check on my progress and handed me a bottle of cold water.

"How are you holding up?" she asked.

"Fine," I lied.

"Good. When you're ready to go on break, make sure you stop in at the Transylvanian Café—you get one meal covered per shift. They make a great Monster Grilled Cheese."

"So I've been told," I said lightly.

She smiled and headed off. The crowds continued to stream into the park, proof that people love to be scared. An hour later, Edie told me to take my break, and I wandered on memory to the restaurant, where the lines for service stretched a dozen bodies deep. I was hungry but decided not to wait. I sat on one of the metal benches outside the Transylvanian Café and gazed around me. Divorce *had* aged me. I wondered how Monsterland would. Thoughts about what I'd seen during the tour threatened to overwhelm me. Frelling's Monster—of all the sights, that one unnerved me most. The creature had no rights, yet was totally innocent of the serial murders. I recalled reading on one of the pages I'd signed or in a brochure in Human Resources that Monsterland didn't exhibit werewolves over human rights concerns—since said werewolves were only, technically, monsters during the nights of the full moon. The rest of the time they were human beings and thus owed fair consideration. But Frelling's Monster was given no such respect.

Around me, the noise of the theme park surged. The clang and clatter of games of chance played in counterpoint to that of the rides. The Dragon Express was in full charge along the upper tracks. From somewhere in that frenetic landscape, a scream rose up. I couldn't tell if it was a woman's or a child's. But I wondered how many children would leave this place only to suffer merciless nightmares as a result of witnessing the reality of monsters.

The monsters *were* real, and they'd been rounded up and confined by the owners of this place.

God help me, I now worked for the monsters that thought they controlled the monsters.

At five, I wandered back to the employee's office and clocked out. The distance to my vehicle seemed more like a gulf of miles—*light-years*. My feet ached along with my back and legs. My first full day on the job had left me wondering how I'd make it through my second.

Still, the crowds streamed in. Bodies lined up to take in the exhibits well before sunset. I plodded out through F-Gate and worried I wouldn't be able to locate my car among the traffic jam. I did. The heap started up without problems. I wanted to let it idle and warm up, but an impatient horn blast from a teen driver desperate for my parking spot got me to pull out before I'd fully removed my Monsterland polo for the old t-shirt meant to disguise my guilt as I was returning to the house on Brunswick Street.

They'd already eaten dinner when I walked through the door. My brother, Linda, and Lonnie lounged in the living room in front of their flat-screen. Vinnie was dressed in his hospital security guard's uniform with its tear-away tie.

"There's dinner on the stove," Linda said, sounding as though she'd rehearsed her delivery.

"Thanks," I said.

"How was it?" asked Vinnie.

"You know, *work*," I said.

I wondered if they might question why I didn't smell like the restaurant I'd claimed to be working at. Not for the first time, I fumed over why Vinnie hadn't put in more of a recommendation for me at the hospital. I'd already concluded that the job was his, and he didn't want me, a screw-up, screwing it up for him. And I was mostly okay with that, though at that moment hurt as well.

Tinfoil covered a pair of shriveled up hot dogs and a dose of macaroni salad from the same deli as the previous night's potato slop. I doused the dogs in mustard, poured myself a glass of water from the tap, and ate alone at the dinner table. After cleaning up, I showered and retreated to the basement rec room, where sleep instantly claimed me.

I drove with the windows down and the radio's volume cranked up. Something old and riveting by Tom Petty blasted out of the speakers. The morning had broken gray and noticeably colder than the recent string of spring beauties, and I was feeling the previous day's long hours in my legs. But the music helped me to ignore it. That and a breakfast of aspirin.

I turned down the road to Monsterland and passed beneath the shadowy cathedral formed by the pines. The Hum's unwanted slithers resumed. I'd get used to it, they promised. I wasn't there yet.

Unlike the last time I'd been here, the parking lot was a ghost town. Food wrappers and other trash littered the pavement. I parked and got out. On my way toward the front gate, a voice called my name. I turned to see Curtis Nesbitt the Third hurrying to catch up to me.

"Morning," he said.

I gave him a tip of my chin in acknowledgment.

"Was hoping to see a familiar face," Curtis said.

"Why's that?"

"I dunno. Still got the jeebs, I guess. You know, this whole *monster* thing."

I chuckled but continued forward. "If working here gives you the jeebs, maybe it's the wrong career path."

"Maybe. What about you?"

"What about me?"

"You were pretty fired up yesterday over Frelling's Monster."

"I just don't think it's right that we, meaning people in general, judge him as not being human enough to be treated fairly, that's all."

"You're probably right," Curtis said.

"First time for everything."

We passed through F-Gate. From there, it was on to the employees' office.

"Why does Wolcotte call you Smith?" Curtis pressed.

"That? Just some misunderstanding," I said.

Curtis snorted a sarcastic laugh. "I think there's a lot of that in his case."

I punched my time card. "Oh, go easy on Bo. The wolves in the wild that raised him did their best."

Martine soon joined us, and again we received our banal newbie assignments. My first duty of the day was to check all of the garbage receptacles and, if they were more than a third full, replace the bags. It was grunt work—the dues I'd be forced to pay before moving any higher in the organization. And I was okay with it, mostly. I wasn't sure I wanted to go higher. I didn't want the responsibility of operating one of the rides. I didn't want to work in any of the park's kitchens or have the stress of preparing food for impatient customers. More so, the idea of having any contact with the park's monsters made me clench in places no adult male should ever feel clenched. Feeding the sasquatches? Worse, the baroness and her brood…

I pulled out a garbage bag half full and crawling with flies. It struck me that I never saw birds here or any other forms of life, only people and flies. Was it the Hum? Flies either tolerated the echo or were actually drawn to it.

The garbage reeked of something rotten. I held my breath, tied the bag shut, and heard the angry buzz of all those who'd been trapped inside. I tossed the bag into the rolling cart I'd lugged through much of the park and pushed on to the next receptacle in line.

I wheeled the cart to a row of dumpsters located out of sight in a corner behind the Human Resources building. Those dumpsters faced a big security gate that was kept locked except when the garbage trucks came to empty them.

I slid back the cover and tossed in bags, nose held, wondering if G.I. Bo hadn't pulled the luckier shit assignment cleaning toilets. If you took the monsters out of the equation, mine was one of those crap jobs teens were sentenced to during summers in high school. *Seasonal work*, my inner critic said. No different than flipping burgers or raking lawns. I was even wearing the embarrassing uniform shirt to prove it.

The first garbage bags struck with a deep *clang*—the dumpster had recently been emptied according to that hollow impact. The fourth or fifth bag I tossed in hit something solid. I swore I heard a gasp that didn't sound as much like trash bags settling as a human being clouted by falling garbage.

I straightened, froze. "Hmmm," I grunted.

Then, lightning-quick, a figure was scrambling through the opening in the side of the dumpster. The sheer madness of such a thing caught me by such surprise that I just stood there while the body maneuvered out of hiding and into the overcast day.

"Who—?" I got out before the shadow clocked me.

I'm no slouch, but the unexpected brunt of the blow to my chin knocked me back. An instant later, I saw a blue-white spark, then searing agony exploded across my right flank. I babbled out something unintelligible before everything sent dark.

When I woke up, my black Monsterland polo shirt was gone along with my ID. The pavement lay hard beneath my cheek. An iron tang of blood coated my taste buds. From the sting, I gathered I'd bitten my tongue when the figure from the dumpster zapped me.

A deceptive calm hung over the day, silent save for the low moan of the wind and the background tremor of the Hum.

Tasered, my dazed senses realized.

I rolled over and looked down at my naked chest. I was in great physical shape, but my first instinct was to cover both of my nipples with my hands. The mark where I'd taken the jolt flamed red on my side. I swore, picked myself up, and suffered a brief but intense spell of vertigo.

I swore again. Someone had broken into the park, stolen my shirt and ID—the latter two crimes, no doubt, for a disguise. My jaw ached, my flank stung, and I'd gnawed off the tip of my tongue in the bargain, judging from the pain. I should have turned in the direction of F-Gate and run hell for my car. Instead, idiot company boy that I'd become seemingly overnight, I headed in the direction where I thought I'd find help.

Rounding the Human Relations building, I pushed open the front door. The chubby receptionist with the dark hair and glasses looked at me with a practiced smile that quickly grew lunatic in appearance.

"There's an intruder in the park," I blathered out of breath, my mouth feeling like it was full of dry cotton. "Has my shirt and ID badge. Tasered me, too—he's armed!"

The receptionist blinked herself out of the trance and calmly turned to her keyboard. A few deft taps, and she said, "According to your last use of your ID badge five minutes ago, you're at Frelling's Castle."

"Contact security," I barked. "Raise the alarm! *Red alert!*" I didn't know what I was saying. Or doing, apparently. Because I turned and beat feet in the direction of Frelling's Castle wherein the real-life Frankenstein monster was imprisoned.

Something over my head sounded in warning—three sharp squawks that clawed at my ears. A muffled shout of voices over the park's loudspeakers followed. Frelling's Castle loomed ahead of me. By that point, I was frantic, consumed by a mix of revenge against the shadow figure that had bested me and concern for the well being of the creature beyond those doors.

I pushed into the lobby. The inner doors leading to the theater beyond stood open—and my stolen ID had likely been responsible. The red light glowed over my head like a silent alarm. I attempted to decelerate. On the last sprint to and through those doors, it struck me that I was in no better position against my mysterious opponent, the dumpster diver, than when I'd first encountered him. He was armed. I wasn't. I couldn't even access whatever safeguards were provided in the lockbox in defense against Frelling's Monster because he had my ID.

As though to cement this point, I nearly stumbled over one of two prone bodies slumped inelegantly just inside those opened doors as I skidded to a halt and what remained of my smarts kicked in. In the poor illumination, I made out their black Monsterland polo shirts and khaki slacks—security guards. A faint whiff of ozone and char carried in the antiseptic air. They, too, had been zapped. I knelt down and checked necks for pulses. They both had them. My eyes darted to the stage. No Frelling's Monster sat on the funched covers of the cot. I stood, shaky. A few steps closer revealed the ankle cuffs were empty.

The monster had been set free!

All the moisture drained from my mouth. The cool air inside the theater prickled across my naked chest. The stillness of my surroundings pressed down with a heaviness that suggested the entire world was holding its breath.

Creak.

The footstep sounded directly behind me. I whirled, expecting to see the interloper wearing my shirt. But the phantom in the dark theater was much bigger and far less athletic than my attacker. Frelling's Monster lurked unchained less than two yards from me. In that moment, I remembered the insurance contract I'd signed just one day before and figured my brother was soon to become quite the wealthy man.

"Uh," I stammered. "Hello."

The creature stitched together from spare body parts stopped its advance, a hand extended menacingly toward me. Its one bad eye fixed me with malevolence. Its good eye seemed to soften in recognition.

"*You,*" the monster growled in a deep tenor voice.

"Remember me?" I asked, adding a chuckle that sounded desperate and quite stupid to my own ear.

"Yes," the creature said. "*Friend.*"

I puffed out another laugh. "Yeah, that's right, I'm your friend."

The monster lowered his hand and harrumphed.

"Did…did someone let you out of your room?"

Frelling's Creature eyed me. "I'm confused."

I shrugged. "That makes two of us, buddy."

"Buddy?"

"Sure, pal," I said. "The same guy who unlocked your shackles with my ID badge zapped me with some serious voltage. I think my hair's standing up."

I laughed again. Then, so, too, did my new friend, though the sound was sharp on the ear. We were still laughing when a commotion of footsteps pounded out near the prone bodies of the two guards. Both Frelling's Monster and I turned to see a small delegation dressed in black polo shirts and khaki pants enter the theater. Ravi Nakur led them. All were armed with what appeared to be high-tech versions of cattle prods, two with rifles I assumed contained tranquilizer darts.

"*Lowen!*" Ravi shouted.

Frelling's Monster growled and tensed. I held up my hand in protest.

"No, it's okay—we're just talking," I called. And then, to my new friend, I said, "It's okay, right, buddy?"

Frelling's Monster tipped a look at me. "Buddy?"

"Yeah, all right, why don't we get you back to your room—get you comfortable so that nothing else bad happens and no one gets hurt. I'll go with you," I said, the words past my lips before I could trap them or think them clearly through.

Frelling's Monster once more extended a hand, though all menace was gone from the gesture. I saw the large, sallow-skinned fingers shake. For the first time, it struck me that the creature was more child than man. A frightened kid in a body made from mangled pieces. I didn't want to touch that hand, but I didn't have a choice.

"Okay, pal," I said.

Our fingers interlaced. The monster's touch wasn't clammy, as I expected, but warm like any other normal person's hand. He squeezed down—not enough to hurt, though I sensed the superhuman strength he was capable of exhibiting if he wanted to.

Holding my breath, I took my first step toward the stage. Wonder of wonders, Frelling's Monster followed.

"Everything's gonna be all right," I soothed in a gentle voice, hating the lie. That stage was the monster's prison, but it was also his only home. There was that, I supposed.

The ten steps and maybe fifteen seconds to reach the four stairs to the stage dragged out like an hour and gulf of miles. I headed up. Frelling's Monster, still holding onto me, pursued like an obedient toddler. I led him over to the bed and guided him to sit.

"There we go, my friend," I said. I sensed the creature's good eye studying me in those tense moments after he was back on his cot.

"Did she hurt you?" the monster asked.

"*She?*"

"The one who stole your shirt and released my chains."

"*She?* Not until now," I sighed. "Taken down by a girl…*son of a bitch.*"

The monster chortled, and how strange his laughter sounded, as though it was the very first time since being brought to life in a fierce lightning storm that he'd truly laughed. I laughed, too.

"You're all right, buddy," I said.

I offered him a high-five. The monster stared at me, suddenly defensive. The threatening nature of the gesture registered and I stepped back. "No, you slap your hand to mine. It means good job. It means…*brotherhood.*"

I moved closer. Frelling's Monster grunted and met my offer with a hard smack that launched me at least two yards across the stage and almost into one of those big tubes that crackled with electricity when switched on.

"Yeah, that's the stuff," I said while shaking out my hand.

From the cut of my eye, I saw Ravi and the small crowd of security guards, who'd grown in number in response to the threat. One carried what I guessed was a flame-thrower, others lethal-looking weaponry that could have fired darts or kilowatts. All studied the action, ready to act.

"Um, buddy," I said. "Is it okay if I put the chains back on you?"

Frelling's Monster's sad gaze narrowed.

"It's just to make sure things are safe," I promised. "That girl who let you out—"

"That girl who stole your shirt," he cut in and chuckled some more.

"Yeah. She wasn't supposed to do either. So what do you say, pal?"

The monster grunted and nodded. I moved back and reached down. Both ankle shackles were a high-tech design held in place by low-tech padlocks, which had been released by my ID and tossed among the chains. Aware of the gallop of my heart, I lowered, worked one cuff back into place and secured it with a padlock. As I was restoring the other around the monster's thick, hairy ankle, he set a hand on my shoulder. I froze.

"You come back?" Frelling's Monster asked.

"Um…"

"And talk with me? Bring me a book to read? I miss reading books," he said.

I laughed in that maniac's voice. "Sure thing. A whole library if you want."

I fastened the other padlock and chanced a look up at the dangerous monster that'd terrified untold legions of park visitors. What I saw in his expression was hope and—dare I think it?—joy.

"You're okay, buddy," I said.

"You, too."

I extended my hand for a shake. Frelling's Monster accepted the gesture.

"*Lowen*," Ravi hissed.

Ignoring him, I rose from my haunches. "Any preference? Mystery? Westerns? Romance?"

But the monster didn't answer. I backed away, reached the stairs, and casually descended. Once there, the concerned monster squad rushed me, and everything that followed was a blur. I again found myself in the exam room at the First Aid Station and shaking like I was in the throes of a fever as the shock passed.

"Here," Ravi said, holding out a shirt for me.

I struggled into the new black polo, which was a size too small and rode above my belly button. Doctor Wandry scribbled on a form—an employee incident report, I guessed.

"How is he?" Ravi asked her.

"*He* is fine," I said.

Ravi waited for the doctor to answer.

"You heard Mister Lowen. Apart from the shakes, he's good. Better than I'd be if I'd gotten Tasered and then stumbled across that monster on the loose!"

I tugged at the hem of my ill-fitting new shirt. "Frelling's Creation isn't a monster—he's a scared child."

"So says you," Ravi grumbled. "That thing's capable of ripping men's arms out of their sockets. You put your life in jeopardy, you know."

Did I know? The trembles suggested I did, but the shakes were subsiding.

"You should have gone for the lockbox," Ravi admonished.

"I didn't have my ID."

"What about the unconscious guards? Did you ever think of taking one of theirs?"

I didn't answer.

"You also did a hell of a job—above and beyond anything I've ever seen from a general hire," Ravi continued.

"Thanks, I think."

"Oh, it was definitely a compliment. For an unskilled worker, you took excellent initiative. Unfortunately, as a result, I'm afraid I'm going to have to fire you."

I stopped tugging at the stupid shirt and faced him. "Excuse me?"

That slippery little smirk was back on the park administrator's face. That frightened me almost as much as my encounter with Frelling's Monster. "Doctor, if you wouldn't mind," Ravi said.

Doctor Wandry gripped her chart and got the hint. "Sure thing." She exited the room.

Ravi waited until the door was shut, picked up the chair in the corner and then took it backwards in that pose of cowboys, old time police detectives in Film Noir flicks, and other Hollywood bad asses. "I like you, Lowen," he said.

I snorted a humorless laugh. "Can't say the same about you at this very moment in time."

"You misunderstand me. My bad," Ravi said, his eyes on me unblinkingly like one of the Frelling's Monster's and both of the Great Lakester's. "I can't let a man of your abilities take tickets at the front gate or sell cotton candy."

"I need this job," I said in a voice barely there.

"No, you need a better one, and I plan to see that you get it. We have enough lackeys to keep the mundane needs of this park running. What I'm talking is the elite side of things. Something more hands-on."

"Operating the merry-go-round?"

Now it was his turn to snicker, but the laugh quickly shorted out. "Someone broke into this park to create mayhem—oh,

I know, they felt it was their moral duty to release Frelling's Monster from its captivity."

"*Him*—he's a him, not an it."

Ravi waved a hand in dismissal. "The semantics are irrelevant. Ingenious, though, I must admit—they've never done that one before, sneaking in during the garbage pickup."

"Have you found her yet?"

Ravi shook his head slowly from side to side. "We will. Your ID's been flagged and deactivated. We figure the intruder's in hiding and likely plans to sneak out of Monsterland among the crowd, but we have our ways. This isn't the first time some moral zealot's made a bold statement against our industry. It won't be the last, which is where you enter into things now."

All I wanted to do was exit the place.

"I think you're an asset. I saw how you handled not only the monster but yourself."

"I was only trying to do the right thing."

"Anyone else would be in pieces by now," Ravi said. "You might think that Frelling's Monster is some harmless innocent, but there are enough body bags dating back to Geneva to prove you wrong."

I didn't comment.

"We have an impressive pool of talent here at Monsterland," he said, sounding like he was reading from memorized script. "Security, Monster Handlers, crisis experts that work behind the scenes. I'm offering you a chance to join *that* team."

It was everything I didn't want. Then he told me the salary and, idiot that I am, I agreed.

I sat at the table, my shirt an inch up from my pants, both excited by the new contract I'd signed at a decent salary and nauseated because of what that contract meant in terms of added responsibilities. I barely touched the grilled Monster Cheese and cup of blood-red tomato soup in front of me.

Ravi had authorized me to take the rest of the day off with pay. I dunked the point of the sandwich, cut diagonally, into the soup and crunched. The buttery bread and the rich soup tasted spectacular, but my insides were tied in knots.

You'll receive a new uniform, Ravi said in my thoughts. *A hell of an upgrade.*

Outside, visitors flocked to the attractions. Some fired basketballs at hoops for the chance to win cheap prizes. Others shrieked as the Dragon Express completed its chug up the tracks and plunged down, down. Others yet would take their first glimpse at a genuine monster and, for the rest of their lives, suffer nightmares as a result.

I pushed the half of uneaten sandwich and cup of tomato soup away from me. I'd gotten too involved with the job on only my second day of work. I'd become one of those sad fools for which the job was everything, and no home life existed.

Look at you now, my inner critic taunted.

I looked at me now—the rest of the day off with pay, and where was I? At the job killing time. After almost being killed by it.

Voices sounded from the hallway outside the employee break room, one of them too loud to be anyone's other than G. I. Bo's. He strutted in beside a black polo shirt I didn't recognize; another wannabe soldier with a brush-cut and ink on his arms.

"There's the man," Bo said when he saw me sitting at one of the tables alone.

I wanted to be out of there as much as I didn't want to be in my brother's basement rec room. "S'up?" I said and then felt stupid.

"Wassup? *Dude,* I heard you beat down Frankenstein's Monster single-handed!"

"*Frelling's,*" I corrected. "And he isn't a monster, not really."

"It's all over the park," Bo continued. Then he noticed the uneaten half of sandwich. "You mind?"

"No," I said.

He scooped it up along with the soup and helped himself. "Yeah, how you wrangled the monster back into his chains and saved the day!"

Bo ate. His new buddy folded his arms and flashed me a dopey smirk. It was a new war story to be told and retold by warriors who weren't there.

"You should have called us, me and Tommy-boy here would have helped you beat down his monster ass!" Bo hooted.

Tommy-boy made a fist and punched air. You could have cut the testosterone in the room with a knife.

"Next time you feel like being a hero, Smith, you be sure to include us in the mission!"

"Yeah," Tommy-boy said.

They high-fived, somehow without Bo spilling the last of the soup, which he knocked back like a shot.

"You get anything out of it?" Bo asked.

I tugged at the hem of the polo shirt riding over my belly button. "New wardrobe, I hear."

"Bonus?" Tommy-boy asked. "They're supposed to dole out bonuses for work above and beyond normal duties."

"I've been promoted," I said.

Both soldiers straightened, and their dopey grins fell off their expressions.

"Seriously?" Bo growled. "So soon?"

"You asked."

"Good for you, Smith," he said, though his tone didn't match his words.

"I told you—my name isn't Smith."

Bo smacked the back of his free hand against Tommy-boy's washboard abs. "Come on. If we catch the intruder, we'll get promoted, too."

"I'm hungry," Tommy-boy protested.

"Do you want lunch, *soldier*, and to be scrubbing public toilets for the rest of your life, or do you want to be like Smith here, one of the chosen?"

"I want to be a Smith!"

Bo shot the empty soup cup into the trash basket with an elegant basketball dunk. Then he belched, which wasn't nearly as elegant, and they left the break room.

I stood and did the same. By the time I was outside in the overcast of the April afternoon, I'd either forgotten or given up on trying to straighten my shirt. I had a t in the car for my transformation before returning to Brunswick Street. I plodded out the gate and through the crammed parking lot. Shitty weather had done little to keep the hordes away. The entire world seemed determined to break into Monsterland on this day.

I crossed the parking lot and pulled my keys from my pocket. Returning early from the job in the middle of the day would lead to interrogations from both Linda and Vinnie, I knew. Maybe Lonnie, too. I'd come up with some excuse—*they were having the restaurant fumigated.* No matter what I said, Vinnie and especially Linda, perhaps Lonnie, too, would assume I'd gotten fired. I was the no-good relative, the black sheep. My ex, Sherry, was a lush, a user. Somehow, she'd gotten all the friends after our divorce. She'd even gotten my family. Linda and Sherry were friends and still close according to the cutting glances I suffered every time my brother's wife and I were in the same room together.

Raindrops struck the back of my neck and wiggled unpleasantly in the echoes of the Hum. I found my car wedged between a pair of gas-guzzling tanks and squeezed myself inside. Rain splattered the windshield. The car had bottled up a stale smell of sweat mixed with despair. I inserted the key into the ignition and turned. Nothing happened. I tried again. The same. My car had given up the ghost and was dead.

I wanted to cry. Instead, I laughed, because I had no more tears left inside me.

If I started walking, I figured I'd reach Brunswick Street in about two days. The alternative was to beg for a ride from one of my fellow coworkers. I could just imagine the explanation I'd be forced to give if Beauregard T. Wolcotte pulled alongside my brother's house at the curb. I'd need to come up with gas money. I had a ten in my wallet, not much more in my bank account. That might get us halfway there in G.I. Bo's land assault carrier.

Exhaustion threatened to overwhelm me. I settled back, breathing in the despair. I wouldn't kill myself to reach my brother's place because that house wasn't home. And I wouldn't waste my last twenty bucks on gassing up Bo's truck. I remembered something I'd heard or read—maybe it was a bit of Zen found inside a fortune cookie. Something that went…in order to be recreated, you first have to be destroyed. Today made it official. I was at the end of the life I'd known. Perhaps even the one I was trying to rebuild from spare scraps like Frelling's Monster.

I folded my arms, closed my eyes, and slumped against the driver's seat. In that deceptive calm, it struck me I didn't feel fear or crushing disappointment. I felt…*nothing*. Eyes clamped shut, I listened to the patter of the rain and drifted off, more floating than asleep.

My eyes shot open to a crash of thunder.

At first, I wasn't sure where I was. Then recognition dawned. I was in my car. The storm had jumped down from the sky and now hammered against the driver's side door. A shadow crept over the window. It was my attacker from the dumpster come to finish the job. I blinked, and the dark cloud became Frelling's Monster. I jolted behind the wheel. My eyes focused. Ravi Nakur stood outside, the knuckle of his pointer finger rapping on the glass.

"Car problems?" he asked.

Ravi rounded the hood of the car and reached for the passenger's side door handle. The door was still locked. He tried the handle. I didn't release the lock.

"I don't have all day," he said in that imperious tone of a man used to getting his way.

I unlocked the door. Ravi got into the front passenger's seat beside me. He smelled of something sweet and exotic, like mango body scrub mixed with the rain.

"Yeah, car problems," I said.

"So I see."

I nudged my focus over to him. "So now you're watching me?"

"No, I'm watching for whomever broke into this park inside an empty dumpster and released one of my monsters," he said with authority. "Lucky for you, I just happened to notice you stuck here in this shit-box of a car."

"Oh," I said and waited. Nothing. "So, did you find her yet? The intruder?"

He faced out the windshield. "I will, and she'll regret ever setting foot in Monsterland. She'll pay for what she's done."

The chill on my flesh returned. The Hum drew tiny, numerous figure eights across the nape of my neck, my bare arms, and around my exposed belly button. Almost as disturbing was the look I caught in Ravi's eyes as he turned to me, there for a fraction of a second. It was the righteousness I'd seen in Bo only ramped up by a hundred. Rabid, murderous, it scared me more than any interaction with Frelling's Monster.

But then it vanished, or Ravi hid it. A spare, slippery smile broke on his lips. "About the car," he said.

"What about it?"

"I can loan you a set of temporary wheels until you have this lemon fixed or junked and acquire something newer and better."

I snorted a laugh. "Just like that?"

"You're part of Silver Unit now, Lowen. I need you rested and focused, not napping in an old junk car and distracted. I can make the call now. The keys will be waiting for you at the desk in Human Resources. Stick shift or automatic?"

I blinked. "Seriously?"

"Yes, seriously. I think there are two automatic models in the motor pool if you'd prefer."

"No, I meant…you'd hand over the keys to a new company vehicle to me just like that?"

Again, Ravi smiled, and again, I inwardly winced. "I told you—you're an important asset to me."

"I'm not an asset, I'm a person."

"Okay, so you're an important member of my team. My elite team. The Silvers."

"I was only doing what was right. Frelling's Monster was scared."

"But you weren't, and that's why I want you among my finest." Ravi reached into his pocket and withdrew his phone. Eyes narrowed, he tapped at buttons, that spare, smug smile on full display. "There," he announced. "I've just advanced you your first week's salary—plus a suitable bonus for your excellent work this day."

"Bonus?" I parroted.

Ravi studied me. "Yes, a bonus—isn't that what you're supposed to receive for a job above and beyond?"

I recalled Tommy-boy's words in the break room and again sensed that I was being watched and also listened to. Ravi was monitoring all of us.

"The money is in your bank account now. You can pick up the keys to a company loaner in Human Resources. If you want, I can arrange for this set of wheels to be towed and repaired or junked."

Sudden warmth drove out the nagging chill. Money in the bank? A reliable car? The concepts were so wonderful that, at first, I overlooked what accepting them meant—what this might cost me. *Money? A shiny new car?* It struck me that there would be other consequences, these ones homegrown. Arriving to Brunswick Street in a new company car would unleash greater hell than if G.I. Bo had dropped me off. Restaurants operated delivery vans, not luxury vehicles.

"I don't know," I blathered.

"There is another option," Ravi said. "We maintain a few private bungalows for visiting dignitaries—shareholders from the council and their families, mostly. You won't find them on any of the park maps. Quite luxurious. I could authorize you to stay in one while you're training and figuring out the rest."

"Luxury bungalow? How much?"

Again, that smirk. "On the company, Lowen."

He pocketed his phone, opened the door, and stepped out into the gray drizzle. "You tell me what it's gonna be."

He closed the door and started back in the direction of the main gate. I sat frozen, paralyzed by everything I'd been offered.

Maybe Ravi *had* seen something exceptional in me. I was so used to being beaten down, was it possible I hadn't recognized my own value?

I jumped out of my dead ride and hastened to catch up with him. "Ravi," I called.

He kept walking and answered me with his back aimed my way. "Yes, Lowen?"

"These bungalows…they have Wi-Fi?"

The same chubby girl with dark hair and glasses seated behind the desk in Human Resources handed me a digital key card in a paper sleeve. "Congratulations, Mister Lowen—you're in Bungalow Three," she said.

"It's Corey, not Mister Lowen," I said with a smile. "Don't you ever go off duty?"

She laughed. "No."

"So where would I find Bungalow Three?"

She pointed toward a nondescript door at the side of the reception area. "Out there. Take a left at the bamboo. You'll see them, and they're numbered."

The gatekeeper smiled. I thanked her.

"Oh, you're so very welcome," she chirped. And then she leaned forward. "You've really impressed Ravi…and the council, I'd say," she said in a voice not much louder than a whisper. "Not just anyone gets the VIP treatment, only those who've earned it."

I stood there with my too-small shirt riding above my gut. "Cool," I said and then headed out the door and into a courtyard. A portico of wrought iron covered the oasis of pavers and flower boxes. Rain dripped down, its hollow, plunking notes inspiring melancholy. From the direction of the main park, thumping calliope music rose in counterpoint along with the muffled screams of joyful terror by those brave visitors on this stormy night.

I wandered down the path. My mind drifted with my footsteps. I thought about my brother, who I promised myself I'd call once I got settled. And of Frelling's Monster, who seemed to crave my friendship. Sherry could have all those other acquaintances—I had Frelling's Creation! Who else could claim a friend like that?

Farther down the path, I came to a clump of tall, dry stalks barely showing traces of green. Bamboo? I wasn't sure, but I guessed I was in the right place. Turn left at the bamboo. There wasn't anything left of the bamboo. The paved path continued straight along a hedge of arbor vitae. I took two steps forward, stopped, and retraced my footfalls to the bamboo.

A paved path that hadn't been there before—or so I swore—now *was*. I looked up. The path meandered through topiaries carved into spiral shapes and past a half-dozen single-story bungalows, each with charming little window boxes and welcome mats on their front steps.

The doors all bore brass numbers in Roman numerals. I passed I and II and approached III. I inserted the key card. The door unlocked. I entered.

Two things struck me as I closed the door—the sweet watermelon fragrance of the air freshener plug-in and the sudden switching off of the Monsterland Hum. The change was so dramatic, so noticeable, that I shuddered. Were the bungalows immune from whatever inspired the constant tickle? I spotted an oblong silver detail embedded in the wooden wall that seemed to vibrate and wondered if it was some kind of force field that absorbed the echo.

The bungalow itself was outfitted like a high-end hotel suite, the kind rich business travelers enjoy. The front room contained an overstuffed sofa and recliner, an acre of flat-screen bolted to the wall, and opened into a kitchenette. In there, I found the fridge well-stocked with designer water, a bottle of wine, another of champagne, fresh fruit, breads, butter, and cold cuts. A gift basket on the counter tied in silver ribbon contained gourmet jams, cookies, and assorted nuts. There was plenty of coffee in the cabinet. I was set.

The bathroom also welcomed me with a gift basket—this one boasting fancy soaps, lotions, and shampoo. Fluffy, clean towels filled a grapevine basket. The toilet paper was two-ply.

I entered the bedroom and tested the mattress. The bed was beyond comfortable and threatened to seduce me within seconds after I sat on the edge. The mattress had controls for heat and coolness. The pillows, all six of them, were like clouds. Another large television was positioned across from the bed at the perfect height. A criminally luxurious white bathrobe with a little black cartoon bat on the upper right chest was draped over the footboard. Any illusion that I wasn't still deep inside Monsterland ended with that one detail.

That life could change so drastically and quickly robbed the strength from my legs. I stretched out across the bed and fell into the cloud of comfortable pillows.

Call Vinnie, my inner voice reminded.

I promised I would. And what to do with the car? Have it repaired or junk the damn thing? My exhaustion got the best of me. I passed out.

When I woke, it was after dark. An eerie silence pressed against the walls. I checked my phone. The time was late. I hadn't intended to sleep. To my surprise, no texts or voicemails from my brother had come in.

No—*where are you?*

No—*we're worried, please call!*

I tromped out to the kitchenette and opened the gift basket, ripping through the clear, shiny plastic. The first sleeve of cookies was from Germany—with milk chocolate. A luscious taste ignited on my tongue. I munched half a dozen and downed a swig of pretentious bottled water from France.

Nothing? Not even a text? The disappointment in Vinnie I normally kept choked down in my stomach surged up like invisible vomit. I returned to how he hadn't gotten me a job in security at the hospital. I reviewed a mental slideshow of all the times he hadn't said anything when his wife was cutting me down with glances or sharp words. I recalled his scowls, his averting eyes, his superior body language, and all those instances he'd been just too tired from the demands of working third shift to be the brother I'd once known, before our mother passed away.

And I recalled our father and what had happened then.

"If I'm such a burden, bro, let me help you out," I muttered before popping the last of those exquisite cookies from Germany into my mouth.

I paced the small kitchenette and formulated a plan. If Ravi was sincere in his offers, I'd take him up on them. I'd stay in Bungalow Three for as long as possible. I'd use the company car to get around in when I needed to get around. I'd pull my few things out of the basement rec room—if the company ride was an SUV, I might be able to make my move in one trip, two tops.

I recalled what Ravi had said about money in the bank. Leaning my butt against the length of granite countertop, I pulled out my phone and dialed the bank's automated teller system. After four steps of inputting information and following instructions, the female robot voice told me my balance.

I almost dropped the phone.

"Uh…" I gasped aloud.

"To repeat your balance, press one," she prompted.

I pressed one. I hadn't hallucinated the figure. A small fortune had been deposited into my bank account owing to one week's salary in advance and a generous bonus.

I made the automated teller repeat it two more times just to be sure I'd heard it correctly. Then I hung up the phone and plucked an obscenely big and ripe apple from the fridge's crisper. The taste matched the promise. Sweet juice flowed down my chin. I wiped it off with a paper towel from the roll hanging beside the sink. I had enough money to rent my own apartment, put a down payment on a new vehicle, and one other thing—I could throw a few Benjamins at my brother and his wife to thank them for their hospitality, which hadn't been so hospitable when I considered it. At least I wouldn't feel indebted to them any longer. If I moved out, I wouldn't have to keep up the charade of working at a restaurant when I was part of Monsterland's elite Silver Unit.

So a plan was hatched, and not a bad one at that, considering I'd lived mostly in a holding pattern since the divorce. My own place. A new car. A decent salary. American dream, *check!* All I had to do was get through this new training.

A sound reached me through the stillness, a sharp titter of laughter, a woman's. I moved to the nearest window and gazed over at Bungalow Two. The windows over there were lit. Figures moved behind the curtains. It was the source of the sound, and it came again, its origin clear now. That was the only thing missing from my plan, my dream. I would soon have everything but still be alone. Unlike my new neighbors, who tangoed and laughed. VIPs, I assumed. Family or friends of the shareholders, the council the receptionist had referred to. Briefly, I envied them their togetherness.

Then I righted at the window, hungry for the macadamias in the gift basket and thinking I should text my brother out of respect. Only like that couple in the bungalow next door, I found myself no longer alone. Someone had snuck into the room with the silence and stealth of a cat.

And that cat had brought his friends.

Three men, all dressed in formfitting black, came at me. One tossed a punch. I blocked it. Another got me into a body hug. I flipped him over my shoulders and onto the overstuffed sofa. After that, the basic math won out in their favor. One of my attackers clapped cuffs on my wrists. The third slapped duct tape over my mouth. My new friend, the flying trapeze artist, pulled a black hood out of his back pocket and tossed it over my head.

Very little after that seemed real.

So much for your plans, dude, my inner critic taunted as time fell off its normal track and seconds, minutes, and decades got confused.

In a disconnected way, I mentally recorded what followed— how they marched me through a door, the bungalow's front door I assumed, though it could have been some exit I hadn't noticed. Cool night air flowed over my bare arms and tickled my exposed gut. Almost immediately, I suffered the unwanted caress of the Hum crawling across my flesh.

My attackers hustled me along even pavement. Once, I stumbled, but the two ninjas guiding me along caught me without difficulty. The duct tape covering my mouth smothered the rosary of expletives I tried to hurl at them. Rage turned to terror, terror to something that wiggled both hot and cold through me.

Time and space blurred.

"Sit down!" one of my captors barked.

They gave me a shove. I landed in a chair. A brief and paralyzing silence followed. Then, they lifted the hood over my head. I was in a cinderblock room with beige walls. The chair faced a metal door—one that I noticed had no handle.

"Remain seated," a different voice commanded, it was piped over an intercom. I recognized it—Ravi Nakur's!

I did as instructed. Behind me, shadows at the periphery, the men in black uniforms waited. Though I had no way to confirm this, I sensed their tenseness, emanating in invisible waves off their powerful bodies. *Ravi?* What kind of game was he playing with me? I screamed into the gag still clamped over my mouth.

"Relax, Mister Lowen," Ravi said.

I didn't and struggled against the cuffs clamped to my wrists.

"Sit still!" Ravi shouted.

I froze.

"This is the first step of your advanced training. You put up a decent resistance to being captured, which I expected. That's good—you're a fighter at heart. I was right about you."

I mouthed an unflattering comeback that the duct tape mostly rendered untranslatable.

"What happens next is absolutely vital," Ravi continued over the microphone from somewhere out of sight.

My focus drifted toward that door without a knob. It struck me that it also lacked hinges. My terror surged back.

"I suggest you stay perfectly still. Silver Unit, stand ready!"

I started screaming even before the door unlocked and rolled open, revealing darkness beyond. My eyes forgot how to blink. I stared into that void, also forgetting how to breathe. Something indistinct swirled just past the threshold and the glow spilling over from our side of the door. The vagueness stepped into the room, into the light. For a second more, it remained mist. Then it condensed into a woman's shapely legs, torso, breasts, and shoulders. A siren dressed in a low-cut, white top, form-fitting black cigarette pants, heels, and a strand of pearls around her thin neck appeared—a woman with auburn hair, black eyes, and a sharp smile.

God help me, standing directly before my restrained body was none other than the Baroness Ursula van Ullmer, the vampire queen.

I wanted to scream again but forgot how to do that, too.

The baroness slinked a step closer, her heels cutting through drifting fog, her movements elegant, hypnotic, liquid.

"Remember, Highness," Ravi threatened.

The baroness's smirk tightened into a scowl. She shot a hateful glance behind and above me at what I assumed to be the direction of our host, the man responsible for this little meet-and-greet gathering.

"You do as I've instructed, and I'm in a giving vein," Ravi said. "If you deviate from the agreement, my men will unleash the hurt—and what's left of your coven gets pig's blood for a month. Perhaps longer."

She flashed Ravi a death-stare. "Understood," the queen of the vampires said in surrender.

"Good. Now, Mister Lowen, the baroness is going to examine you. Don't be alarmed."

"*Alarmed?*" I shrieked into my gag, punctuating the statement with another round of expletives.

"Just relax. The sooner Her Majesty concludes her examination, the quicker this ends and you return to your bungalow."

Suddenly, she was directly in front of me. Fresh invisible ice formed over my flesh, turning my sweat clammy. In my next shallow sip of breath, I detected her perfume—a faint floral smell of orchids or other exotic flowers. The fragrance struck my senses as *old*, a ghost of something that *once was*. A smell of funerals. Riding beneath it was another, this something foul.

I resisted looking up into the baroness's dark gaze.

"I won't harm you," she said in a sweet, feminine voice tinged in a *soupçon* of Eastern European accent. "I want to. Oh, yes, I'd love to rip out your throat and drink you dry. But I won't."

"*Baroness*," Ravi chastised.

"Very well," she tsked. "Look at me, Mister Lowen."

She'd spoken my name! I jolted my head away. She cupped a hand to my chin, her touch icy, and tipped my face back in her direction. Against my will, I fell into the dark gravitational pull of her eyes, which were still black but also now red around the edges and yellow at their centers.

"Open yourself to me, Mister Lowen," the baroness urged in a seductive voice.

I took a heavy swallow. My saliva tasted sweeter than candy.

Open? I laid it all bare.

How, when making love to my ex-wife the night of our wedding, I'd fantasized about Vinnie's girlfriend, the one before he met Linda, the one whose hair always smelled like strawberry shampoo. I confessed how jealous I was at first when our father grew closer to Vinnie and how afraid of him I became, more so, how afraid of me he got after the incident when the room shook. How nothing I tried to do in penance after that frightening Saturday put me anywhere near my brother's esteem in his eyes. I exhumed the time I wet my pants in second grade, how I'd once stolen money from my mother's purse, covered up the crime of breaking a drinking glass, hated to fill the ice cube trays, didn't like kids—I supposed I loved my nephew Lonnie because he was family, but actually *like* him? No way. I hated his stupid, plastic toys, when he whined, the way he chewed with his mouth open—

"*Focus*," the baroness hissed, squeezing my chin just hard enough that it started to smart. "These are foolish mortal concerns and not why I'm here."

White noise exploded inside my head. "Okay," I mouthed behind the duct tape.

Ravi cut in. "Ask him about the object of interest!"

The baroness cast another hateful glance behind me. Then she again focused on me, and I was spellbound by the electric yellow sparkle within her black eyes. "What do you know of the Abyss?"

"*Abyss?*" I mumbled through a barrier of duct tape.

"Open your mind. Receive the image," she said, her voice so like honey, so undeniable.

Among that white noise, an image did materialize. At first, its outline was indistinct, a blur of gray surrounded by obsidian.

"Do you see it?" she asked from what sounded like a hundred miles away.

I mumbled an affirmative. The blur solidified. What I stared at resembled a brain, gray and crenulated. It hung suspended over a stone slab and the darkness I thought was surrounding it was actually leaking out of the folds.

Curious, she said. It took me another second to realize her lips hadn't moved. The baroness was speaking in my thoughts, one-on-one, only to me.

"What?" I asked into my gag.

You made the room shake?

The vision of the giant gray brain oozing blackness through its crenulations wavered. For a terrible moment, I was there again. It was a Saturday morning, a week after my mother died. The sharp smell of pine cleaner hit me so clearly that it could have been that morning, not this night nearly twenty years later. My father sat in his recliner, his feet kicked up, the bottoms of his white crew socks dirty with sweat or grime, a beer bottle in his hand. Someone had volunteered to clean up the place, a neighbor's wife, the one with the short blonde hair—her name, I couldn't recall it as the vision surrounded me…*us*, because the baroness was there watching, too.

The pine cleaner, almost too thick to breathe…my mother dead, my father seated there, drinking his beer, alive. And then the room began to shake, the bottle in his hand to slosh its contents, the deafening thunder-crack as glass splintered, some of it cutting his palm, and the way he looked at me as pictures jumped off nails and slid down walls and things toppled.

There's a switch inside your head, stuck between positions, the baroness said clearly, and that old image shorted out, replaced once more by the one I was meant to see. *I can try to flip it fully open, but that might kill you.*

"Please, don't," I mouthed. "No, please."

"Baroness," Ravi said.

Her sharp smile tightened in front of me. "Do you see the Abyss?" she said for his benefit.

I nodded.

Good, Now, are you able to see down? Inside the grooves at what's hidden there?

I peered closer. Beyond the dark miasma of the crenulations, an indigo light pulsed through a fibrous veil. And among that light, I saw movement. Something skittered between the flashes.

"Is he—?" Ravi asked, and the vision threatened to shatter.

"Quiet, *idiot!*" the baroness snapped.

I imagined Ravi stewing in whatever protected enclave he gave orders from. He wasn't a man used to being talked down to, especially by one of his monsters.

The baroness's eyes loomed behind the vision. *Concentrate,* she said. The gray brain wavered before stabilizing. *Mister Lowen, you are looking at the Abyss,* she said in my thoughts.

Don't you mean looking into *the Abyss?* my inner jokester fired back. How brave of me to bandy words with the murderous queen of the vampires like we were discussing the weather.

Silence! Pay attention! Your very life depends upon the answers you give.

Sorry.

You see what's inside, the true nature of the evil from the stars, she said.

I peered into the crenulations, past the fibrous membrane, the indigo light show, and at the writhing thing within. *Yes.*

Given what I know about you—about how you made the room shake, you should be able to touch it. Can you touch it, Mister Lowen?

Uh...

Try. Attempt to reach into the carapace with your thoughts.

I don't want to, I fired back.

She huffed out something in a harsh language that sounded like she was hacking up a hairball before stating, *I don't want to be here with you, the Four Seasons are playing on the turntable back in the enclosure. But I don't have a say in the matter—if I want human blood instead of swine thanks to your new bosses. And neither do you, so please try!*

I willed a cerebral version of my hands in front of me. They appeared in the vision. My real hands attempted to break their bonds. To my embarrassment, shifting in place, I found that I'd gotten erect. Uncomfortably so.

That's it, Ursula van Ullmer cooed, which added to and likely caused my condition. *But there's something else you should know.*

My imaginary fingers reached the imaginary carapace. Pain surged through me, cold and electric, similar to that jolt you feel from getting zapped by a faulty plug on a small appliance. Only it was worse, much worse. It scattered my thoughts, made my teeth chatter, and put me back in the second grade, my bladder cramped and ready to explode.

Yes, that, the baroness said. *What you're suffering is the mortal, human reaction to the Abyss. A single second is pure misery. By the third or fourth, it might drive you insane. Unless you can grab hold of it and put it to sleep. Unless you make it your bitch.*

Nothing she said registered or made sense. Through the indigo glare, I looked down to see that my hands *had* penetrated the crenulations and fibers. What I held felt slick and frigid, like something dead that had washed up on the beach. Only that ocean corpse wasn't dead. It wiggled in my grasp. I managed to hold onto it for another second, somehow aware of its rage and also its panic. It snapped free of my clutches. My fingers and palm ached, as though they'd been burned or frozen.

Impressive, the baroness said. Her eyes were in front of me, still malevolent but soft with surprise.

"Well?" Ravi demanded.

The baroness stared. Under her scrutiny, I agreed that, vampire queen or not, she was stunning.

Thank you, Lowen, she whispered in my thoughts. *I am stunning.*

The room around me blurred. I heard Ravi barking for an update. The baroness continued her study of me.

"No, Mister Nakur, he wasn't able to penetrate the Abyss's keep-stone or put it to sleep," she lied. *Trust me, you don't want him to know that you did,* she spoke in my thoughts. *You did an impressive job. Best to keep that a secret, Lowen.*

Ravi swore. "Fine. Remove the memory from his consciousness so he doesn't go crazy."

The barest curl of a smile twisted on the baroness's lips. "Of course."

She leaned closer, and to my shock, all I could think about was what it would be like to kiss that mouth. A disgusting urge, I know, considering how many throats that mouth had ripped out over the centuries. Her lips were stained with the blood of countless victims. And pig's blood, too, when she didn't capitulate to Ravi's demands.

Don't forget. Remember that you've seen the Abyss—the other monster they've imprisoned here within these walls. You will suffer the worse nightmares of your life as a result, because you've looked deep into it, touched it. But if you forget, you'll also forget what you were forced to do on this night, and it's better that you remember what's happening around you, Lowen.

"It's done," she said and straightened, giving me a knowing look along with a wink—that, too, supremely arousing.

I hung my head. It seemed the right course of action.

The door through which she'd come again whisked open.

"You can return to your psychedelic party pad, Your Highness," Ravi said. "As agreed, several IV bags full of human red corpuscles will be delivered within the hour."

She shot an icy stare over me and at the rear of the room beyond my line of sight. Then the baroness turned. The action unleashed several swirls of mist. I blinked, and she was gone. The door sealed into its frame.

"Release him," Ravi said.

One of the soldiers ripped the duct tape off my yap. Another, a man with a scar running down one cheek, removed his ID and swiped it to unlock my cuffs. I shifted in the chair, still hard—a fact not lost on my captors.

Scarface snickered. "Someone's in love."

I ignored him. The Abyss. A monster from the stars, and one not on any of the park's maps. A horror not sold in cuddly stuffed animal form in the gift shop. I wasn't supposed to remember it. But I did. I was brought here to try to grab hold of it and put the monster to sleep. I had. I wanted to sock Scarface on his other cheek.

I did and landed a solid uppercut.

I jumped up. Dizziness—maybe the ferocity of my erection—sent the world into a spin.

"That's enough," Ravi snapped.

I shook out my hand and whirled on him, ready to launch another knuckle sandwich at his face. Ravi caught my fist in mid-swing, stopped it dead, and lowered it with unexpected ease.

"I said that's enough," Ravi growled.

Chest heaving, I looked around me. Behind the chair was a small booth, one likely well-armed with wards and other protections. Ravi's very own private seat for whatever carnage got performed in this room.

"Let me guess," I huffed. "I was never in any true danger, is that it?"

All three of the guards lingered close by me, with Scarface the nearest.

"Oh, the only time you've come closer to death was with Frelling's Monster," Ravi said dryly. "At any moment, the baroness could have ripped out your throat."

I made another foolish charge at him. The uniforms held me back, though from his earlier block, it was clear that Ravi Nakur could hold his own—against mortals, at least.

"Welcome to the Silvers, Lowen. That's what every night on the job is going to be like. This was a test. I'd give you a B-minus. And if you ever come at me like that again, you'll find I'm just as dangerous as any monster in the park." Ravi nodded at Scarface. "Escort Mister Lowen back to his accommodations if you would, Urbino."

"Yes, Mister Nakur," Scarface said.

The man reached for me. I held up both hands in warning. "Lead the way."

The one named Urbino waved me toward the exit. I walked ahead of him.

"Oh, Mister Lowen," Ravi called.

I stopped but didn't turn around. "Yeah?"

"What did you think of it?"

"It? Don't you mean *her*?"

"Not the baroness, the Abyss."

"Abyss?" I parroted.

But Ravi said no more, and Urbino nudged me along. I wandered through the cinderblock hallway toward a security door. Urbino used his ID badge to deactivate the alarm. We emerged into a cool, damp night at the rear of the vampire exhibit, a part of the park not accessible by tourists.

An eerie silence hung over Monsterland. The park was closed, the visitors all gone. So, too, were the grunts that sold armbands and corn dogs and swept up food wrappers. The only souls here belonged to elite soldiers and the cursed.

"*Left*," Urbino growled.

"I know the way," I spat back.

"Just wouldn't want you to get lost," he snickered.

Lost? The job had become more, so much more, than I'd ever imagined while attending the fair. Then, I hadn't had much of a trajectory other than to earn a paycheck. I'd been trapped in my brother's basement rec room, driving a car that was on its last legs, and alone. In an instant, I now had money, access to a new set of wheels, and my own luxury living space. I even had a friend in Frelling's Monster. On paper, in bare terms, I'd found something— a new direction, a new life.

But at what cost?

We trudged through the park, passing beneath the glow of lamps and then into long stretches of darkness. The remains of my erection, pinned at an awkward angle in my khakis, complained the entire distance. Finally, we reached the Human Resources building. I entered the courtyard. My chaperone followed.

"I'm good," I said.

He stepped closer.

"Really, dude—*Urbino*, is it? I can take it from here."

"We're not done yet."

"We aren't?"

I wandered past the bamboo stalks, backtracked, and found the path that hadn't been there the first time. At the door to Bungalow Three, I remembered my key card. As though reading my mind like the baroness, Urbino withdrew the card and offered it between two black-gloved fingers.

I snatched it out of his clutches and opened the door. The place was as I'd left it—macadamias still waiting to be eaten, bathrobe over footboard—but with one alteration. Now, laid out on the bed, was a crisp, black uniform identical to the ones worn by my abductors. A new pair of military boots sat on the floor beside the bed.

"Tomorrow night—*midnight*," Urbino stressed, "meet up at Checkpoint Zero. Also known as the Great Lakester exhibit."

"Okay."

Urbino assessed me through narrowed eyes. "I disagree with Director Nakur."

"You do?"

"B-minus? I'd have given you a D."

I shrugged off the snipe. "This D managed to clock your ugly puss after being messed with by the vampire queen. Doesn't that at least earn me a D-plus?"

Urbino snorted in response and wordlessly departed. In the wake of the door closing, I again broke into the shakes. I couldn't tell if it was over my encounter with the baroness so up close and personal, my trip into the past—for a shocking moment, the sharp tang of pine cleaner filled my nose—or that other player in this matter of monsters.

The Abyss.

Monsterland had another horror imprisoned, this one out of view by all save a handful of shadow agents. A monster from the stars? Grab hold of it? Put it to sleep? I had done that more with my mind than my hands. I wiped my palms on my pants. What was that thing? B-minus? Ravi and the others didn't know I'd earned a solid A.

But they couldn't know that, according to the queen of the vampires. Was she now a new friend? That was doubtful. Perhaps an ally in whatever shit show I'd landed in.

I didn't drink, not anymore, not since the divorce. Still quivering, I popped open the champagne and swallowed a hearty pull. The bubbles surged down my throat and threatened to claw their way back up on a geyser of puke. Somehow, I held in the contents of my stomach. Even managed to pass out in my new, comfortable bed at just after three in the morning.

The baroness warned that there would be nightmares. But it wasn't night when I suffered through the first of them. A bright morning had dawned beyond the bungalow's curtains, I discovered through wide-open eyes after jolting upright in an unfamiliar though criminally soft bed.

The Abyss…it had spoken my name. My full name. Even my middle one—*Irvin*. And it had done so in a genderless child's cackle. You'd think something so evil would address you in a booming baritone, not a giddy falsetto. That made it worse.

Soaked in sweat, I sucked down a breath that refused to come easily. For a terrible instant, it seemed to be in the room with me, out of focus, lurking behind the curtains, the robe at the foot of the bed, my new Silver Unit uniform now hanging off the top of the bedroom door's frame, and in every corner. But as daylight registered, the dream evaporated.

I showered, using some of that high-end swag from the gift basket then dressed in my clothes from the day before, which had acquired some funk. The black polo shirt rode an inch higher up my stomach, I swore. Then I set out to the front desk in Human

Resources, where the chubby girl with the dark hair and glasses told me a car was waiting at my disposal.

The car was parked just outside the front gate—that year's model of a luxury SUV. It was trappings like this and the high thread count of the sheets that made me momentarily overlook being kidnapped and laid bare to the queen of the vampires.

My old car was gone, likely to be junked. That Ravi Nakur didn't miss much in terms of details. My new set of loaned wheels was all push-button. I pushed a button to start her up. The transmission had advanced beyond a stick shift—all the gears were buttons displayed on the dash and located to the direct right of the steering wheel.

I even found a pair of shades secured to the visor. They suited me. Not bad for a B-minus, I agreed, and, with a full tank of gas, drove out of the park at just after nine on a sunny spring morning.

I was halfway to Brunswick Street before I remembered the radio, which was connected to satellite, and got some nine trillion channels. The wind washed in through the open driver's side window, sweet in a way that only spring is. I'd gotten lost in my thoughts. Okay, I needed new clothes. And I'd promised Frelling's Monster that I'd read to him. I'd pack clothes and a few books when I reached the house.

I flipped through the radio, scrolled along half a billion channels, and settled on classic rock. Something old by the Doobie Brothers poured out of the sound system. Elegant, I could almost remember the lyrics. Hadn't heard them since high school. A party in tenth or eleventh grade. The musical selection that night had been old classics and modern hip-hop. I'd dug the classics.

To my shock, the baroness's face appeared in my mind's eye. She was a killer, a monster, but she was also a beauty, timeless in that attraction. *Lowen,* I heard her say from our encounter in the secret interrogation chamber.

I choked down a dry swallow. My inner critic reminded me that the baroness wasn't likely so damn attractive when her fangs had sunk into a victim's throat or when she was ripping out hearts with her taloned, bare fingers.

The lightness of my morning vanished. I recalled Ravi and the ease in which he'd stopped my punch dead in the air, the duplicity of the baroness, and the little I knew about the Abyss. I'd grabbed hold of the monster—for at least a few seconds. Why was that important, and why had the vampire queen warned me to stay silent about that half-thrown switch inside my noggin?

The music about the beliefs of fools continued, not nearly as electrifying. I drove on.

The same sinking emotion weighed down my gut as I turned onto Brunswick Street. Linda's minivan and Vinnie's truck were both parked in the driveway. I imagined Vinnie passed out following his hospital security shift. My pulse raced. I didn't want to be here.

I pulled up to the curb unsure of what to say but knowing I'd be required to offer some explanation. Naïvely, I wondered if I could sneak in and escape unnoticed.

Linda cornered me before I could slip down the stairs to the basement. "Where have you been?" she demanded, her voice a whisper out of respect for her sleeping husband.

I faced her, at first not answering. Where had I been? The answer was none of her business. I stared at her face, which I hated, and understood that I was done living under this roof and her spiteful thumb.

"Work," I said, my voice the temperature of ice.

"If you think you can come and go here like this is some kind of sleazy motel—!"

"No, sleazy motels don't treat you like an unwanted guest," I said and brushed past her to the basement.

"You're a *shit*, Corey Lowen!" she called down at me. "Sherry was too good for a *no-good* piece of shit like you!"

On any other day, her words might have wrought the damage she sought to inflict. Ravi thought I was a B-minus. The baroness, in secret, had informed me I was an A. I'd been offered money, my own place, and luxury wheels—I didn't need to linger here like some sub-human prisoner any more. I wasn't Frelling's Creature or a sasquatch or some mummified relic from Ancient Egypt denied respite. I wasn't a monster, certainly not the kind she'd painted me as.

The faint mildew smell of the basement struck my nose. After a full day away from the house, I sputtered, hating the foulness I'd grown used to as much as Linda's face. My limbs tingled with pins and needles. My lungs ached. My stomach had filled up with broken glass and wasp stingers. For an instant of blinding rage, I didn't know what to do first.

You're moving out, my inner voice said.

Ravi had offered up temporary digs, nothing permanent. But this basement hellhole was also temporary living. He wanted me among his Silver Elite Team. As soon as Ravi asked me to, I'd find a better place than Bungalow Three to inhabit. Until then, it was home.

I grabbed clothes and stuffed them into the garbage bags that had become my luggage. I stacked two at the base of the stairs and then two more, adding my towels and dress shoes and three pairs of sneakers into their maws.

I had plastic tubs and cardboard boxes, about a dozen, stacked atop the dry bar. The SUV could just about handle all of it if I was scientific about things. One of those boxes contained a pair of old sports trophies from high school. Was it any great tragedy if they somehow didn't make it out of the rec room with me? No, they were mine—I was taking them with me. I'd make it all fit.

I trudged up the stairs with one box and one bag full of clothes. Her Eminence, my brother's wife, stewed somewhere out of view. I'd gotten all four bags onto the back seat and an equal number of boxes of my things into the rear hatch when my brother appeared, his hair a mess of bed-head, barefoot, clad only in flannel PJ bottoms and a ripped t-shirt bearing the logo of the local Major League Baseball team.

"What are you doing?" he didn't so much ask as insist.

"What does it look like?" I responded and continued on down to the basement for my next haul.

It was clear that Vinnie had just woken up—or, more to the point, that he'd *been* woken up by his wife. He padded down the carpeted stairs right as I lifted two of the remaining boxes from the diminishing pile of my life's relics.

"Hold on," he said, again in that imperious, big brother tone.

I moved past him and back up the stairs. When I returned to the basement, Vinnie stood with his arms crossed over his chest, his body langue impossible to misread.

"What's going on, Corey?" he asked, this time in the form of an actual question.

"Isn't it obvious? I'm moving out."

"Out? To where?"

I huffed in response and reached for two more boxes. The one on top sported those stupid trophies.

"Bro," he said.

Was that actual concern I heard? I hesitated. "You don't have to put up with me around here any longer. I've got my own place now."

"Where?"

"At work. They've got a space for me. It's mine for as long as I need it."

"A space? At this restaurant?"

Not sure why, I came clean and smoothed down my rumpled and ill-fitting polo shirt. Vinnie's bleary eyes took in the cartoon vampire bat.

"I didn't get hired at some shitty restaurant. I'm working at Monsterland, the theme park."

Vinnie fixed me with a look that suggested he thought he was still asleep and had dreamed my revelation. "Monsterland. With the monsters. *Are you nuts?"*

Our brief moment of brotherhood had ended. "Monsterland beats the ones here," I said and resumed my escape.

I foisted the two boxes into the rear of the SUV. When I returned to the front steps, the last of my things had been carried up the stairs and deposited there.

Message received.

I drove away feeling liberated. The music regained its punch, the morning its joy. I hit the drive-through ATM at my bank and withdrew a few hundred dollars. My wallet hadn't been that thick in months. I pulled into a restaurant parking lot, entered, and took a table for one. I ordered a fat prime rib steak and fries, which I doused with salt and ketchup. Even asked for chocolate cream pie for dessert and ate it all. I left a generous tip, donned my shades, and motored back to Monsterland.

Passing through the cathedral of tall pines, I felt the stirring of the Hum, heard some distant screams that could have been from happiness or terror, and understood that I had committed. I was all in now. There was no turning around.

I carried one box and one bag through F-Gate. The black polo shirt on duty arranged for me to borrow a cart, which made things a hell of a lot easier. I unloaded the SUV in three trips and stacked my belongings along one wall in the bedroom.

At three o'clock, I put my head down. Sleep claimed me, and I dreamed of the Abyss.

It spoke to me in Lonnie's voice. It took on my nephew's face. The boy-creature's eyes glowed a vibrant, diseased indigo. "Do you know who I am?" the thing asked.

"You're the Abyss," I answered.

The horror chuckled. "No, I'm your nephew."

"You most certainly *aren't.*"

"Great grammar, uncle."

"Don't call me that. My nephew has his mother's cruel eyes. Shit-brown ones."

The thing stared, mouth agape. More indigo light pooled where other kids had throats. "You're mean."

"Just telling it like it is."

"I'm just a kid. You tried to hurt me. Next time, I'll hurt you."

"What makes you think there'll be a next time?"

The thing wearing my nephew as a disguise flashed a look of evil so malevolent, my balls shriveled. The indigo in its eyes turned black. Its mouth opened, revealing an abyss.

"Oh, we'll meet again, Uncle Corey," it said in that alien falsetto. "And when we do…"

I jolted awake, the scream clogging in my throat. What I saw in that last second was so horrific that my mind blanked it out.

I showered again—not because I needed to but to unknot my muscles. I'd woken up so tense that everything ached. The hot water helped to relax me. The Abyss. Baroness von Ullmer had warned me about nightmares. The ending of this one was quite possibly the worst I'd ever suffered. It ranked up there with the real-deal shaking of the room on that Saturday morning and the explosion of my father's green glass beer bottle from a moment in time when everything changed in terms of ugliness.

The Abyss knew who I was. The Abyss had gotten into my head. I shuddered beneath the steamy spray.

"It was only a dream," I said aloud and tried my best to believe it as I toweled dry.

As I pulled on the black uniform, I discovered what made it different from the flimsy, black polo shirts worn by the day Monsterlanders. Stitched into the upper right chest was a rectangle of metal. A smaller version of the piece fit into the bungalow's wall was secreted into the shirt. A ward?

I wandered through the silent park, aware of not only the absence of visitors but also of the Hum. Despite what Martine had promised us, I hadn't gotten used to the slither and echo or how they made my ears itch. Was it possible the Hum was set to a timer like lights and other fixtures in the park? No, I realized it was the new uniform's doing. I reached the main thoroughfare and paused, ran my thumb over the oblong piece of metal sewn into the uniform's shirt, and received a tiny zap from contact with the ward. I didn't touch it again.

The giant aquarium tank rose ahead of me. My heart resumed its gallop. It could have been the desolate nightscape of Monsterland, the nightmare, or the occupant of the colossal fish tank that quickened my pulse. Four men in similar uniforms stood beneath the too-white glare of lights. I joined them three minutes before midnight.

"You're here," Urbino said.

"Did you think I wouldn't be?" I clapped back.

"Naw, I figured you'd bolt after last night with the vampire. I see I gave you credit for more brains than you have—that you're too stupid to know you shouldn't be here."

I laughed. "Good to see you, too."

Urbino smiled, a grisly expression that belonged on some rabid animal's face. "Come on."

After brief, official introductions—all of my fellow Silvers, culprits in my previous night's abduction—we jogged like military cadets behind Urbino to the first of our duties: the sasquatch enclosure. At night, the trees inside the electrified pen were all monsters waiting to grab at us and crack our bones.

"This is the opening stop of a very long work shift," Urbino said. "Men, this newbie in your uniform needs to learn what we do here after hours; what it's like to be a true Silver."

I waited, saying nothing.

"He's no Silver, Knuckles," another of my fellow warriors said.

"Not yet," said Urbino.

"*Knuckles?*" I said.

The uniform who'd insulted me stepped forward, chest puffed up. "You're looking at Knuckles Urbino, the man who put an end to the baroness's reign of terror and captured her for display at Monsterland, *meat.*"

"Hi, my name is Corey Lowen, not 'meat' and I didn't know I was being trained by a bona fide celebrity!"

I extended my hand. The other uniform laughed in dismissal and cut me through with a look. I knew what they were doing, the tactic of insults and intimidation meant to put me in a very humble role as the newest trainee in their private little army. What they didn't realize was that after living with Sherry and then Linda, I was beyond being humiliated and intimidated.

"Okay, so what now?" I asked.

It turned out that we were there to feed and clean up after the family of four that lived among those nightmare trees. A cart identical to the one I'd used to unload my things from the SUV rolled up to the enclave, pushed by a dude clad in the daytime garb of khakis and black polo shirt. The cart carried three tubs. Inside each were mushrooms. I caught the earthy, funky smell of the pallid things as they passed by me.

"They eat mushrooms?" I asked.

"No, they eat people. But unless you're volunteering…" Knuckles Urbino said.

Feeding the sasquatches was a delicate, coordinated act. The only way in and out of the enclosure was a secured door forbidden to the public. Knuckles Urbino stood at the keypad that activated not only the door but also other controls. As he explained in a condescending manner, once he deactivated the charge, the inhabitants inside the pen would be on the move. He would then initiate a sonic pulse, one that would drive them back long enough for the pen to be cleaned and the food laid down. Our job was to get in and out as quickly as possible. Sweep, dump, and run, in other words. I picked up one of the bins of mushrooms and held my nose.

"Uh, nuh-uh," my new buddy and fellow Silver, Jody Baxter, said. He relieved me of the tub and handed me a small rake and scoop.

"Fine. I'm more of a pepperoni on my pizza kinda guy than mushroom anyway," I joked. Oh, that Corey Lowen—so funny!

Urbino hit the charge, and we all felt it. The security door rolled open. At the far back of the procession, I followed my three fellow Monsterlanders-in-all-black inside. Urbino switched on the floodlights and also the eclipse-thing that made Big Momma, Big Daddy, Junior, and Uncle Lou visible. Ahead of me, the first of the uniforms dumped the contents of his bin. The second followed suit. I did my best to scoop up sasquatch scat, of which there was plenty, trying to work fast. For my first time, I think I did a decent job. The third uniform emptied his tub of mushrooms and barked at me to hustle.

"*Faster, Lowen,*" Knuckles Urbino shouted, adding to the urgency.

I stepped through the door. Urbino flipped a switch. From the cut of my eye, I noticed a hand drawing back, only inches away from me in the stark white glare of the spotlights. The one named Uncle Lou had almost grabbed hold of me. The door slammed into place. The current again flowed.

"What the hell—?" I spat.

To this, Urbino and the others chuckled. Past them, in the enclosure, the sound of rigorous chomping issued forth. In that last moment before the eclipse fully faded and their extra natural camouflage again kicked in, I saw all four residents stuffing their faces with mushrooms.

From there, we jogged to the mummy exhibit. In the overcast of night, the exterior struck me as a view into the real Valley of Kings, a land of mysteries and ancient magic. My skin still prickled from my close call with Uncle Lou, but I was moving on automatic, going through the motions wearing a pair of those old blinders they used to put on horses to keep them focused on the task at hand. Mine were mostly invisible.

I didn't think that mummies ate anything. Other than the ceremonial headdress Urbino had me don, this part of the night's duties seemed the easiest.

"Really?" I asked.

"Really."

The thing looked to be made of real gold and came to a point in the center of my forehead with a jeweled snake. No, an *asp*, my inner voice corrected. We were, after all, in a reproduction of the mystical realm of the pharaohs. The asp trailed silk fabric onto my head.

"You look like a pharaoh," Urbino teased.

I felt like an idiot.

"What's this for? To ward off dark spirits? To contain the mummies?"

"Something like that."

We entered the exhibit through the security doors. The air thrummed with an electric undercurrent, but the Hum had vanished from my perception. The atmosphere was thick with a dusty, desert smell. I could almost detect a trace of summer heat— sun baking in the grains of sand. But over that was a pet's terrarium smell, a note of funk from reptiles. The overhead false sunlight glowed. Urbino flipped a switch on the outside keypad and the current crackling through the air shorted out.

"There," he said.

I realized he'd killed the juice that jolted the mummies out of their sarcophagi and into constant motion back and forth across the counterfeit desert sands.

"We're safe," he said.

"Safe?" I asked.

"They only want to sleep. They're *old*," he said. "They really couldn't care less about us or any of this."

Our duties inside the mummy exhibit concerned raking out the tracks pounded into the sand between the two lines of opposing caskets. In this regard, we were more like a baseball ground crew raking the infield after a game. I combed out the sand, aware of the three mummies, each one nestled within the confines of its sarcophagus, bony arms folded over chests in funereal poses, eyes closed. There had been times during the divorce and after in my brother's basement when I'd felt as depleted as the living dead of Ancient Egypt. At that moment, I pitied them—geriatrics yet cursed to a kind of Hell of modern man's making. They only wanted to sleep, but Monsterland denied them that basic right apart from this respite.

"That should do it," Urbino said.

We all headed out through the security door. Then our leader reactivated the electrical zap.

"Can I remove this now?" I asked, indicating the headdress.

Baxter snickered behind me.

"Sure," Urbino said.

I did so and handed him the headdress, which none of my fellow Silvers had donned to enter the mummy exhibit.

"So I take it this had nothing to do with security measures," I said. "Very funny. This is a regular frat house."

The mood at our next stop wasn't nearly as slapstick.

We jogged to the aquarium wherein the Loch Ness horror was housed. Nestor wasn't supernatural but instead preternatural—*extra*-natural. But it was still a monster—and supremely dangerous.

"It's up to us to feed the creature and scrub the tank," Urbino explained, talking down to me in a superior tone that briefly made me flush with hot anger.

"Let me guess—as the new guy, I get to scrub up dinosaur shit, right?"

"No, that's our job. But in order to do that, you'll need to strip out of your uniform."

I did a double take. "Say what?"

"You heard me."

I flashed a stupid grin, still hot, still thinking I was being pranked like with the Egyptian headdress. "You're kidding, right?"

"You can wear your uniform into that water, but I don't recommend it. You'll be dripping wet the rest of your shift."

I glanced around. The looks on the faces of my fellow Silvers told me that Urbino wasn't joking. I wondered if they planned to feed me to the dinosaur—if all the luxury perks I'd experienced over the brief hours of the previous day were some kind of cruel payoff. Then Urbino moved to the enclosure's keypad and lowered the steel cage. It descended from the ceiling. He guided it by the controls onto the platform beside the monster's tank.

"One of us has to act as a decoy while the others wash the tank and release the live food," Urbino said, again using that tone. "Until you're more adept at the rest of the routine, you're bait so we don't wind up being chum."

I stood frozen where I was for five more seconds. "Me? In *there?*"

"You'll be safe. I can almost guarantee it," Urbino said.

The cage was one of those metal fortresses that men lower inside of to swim with great white sharks. And like I imagine with many of those cages, this one was covered in scrapes and tooth marks from what I guessed were quite a big set of teeth.

"Just about?" I huffed and began to strip.

I went down to my boxer-briefs and socks. The chilly, damp atmosphere inside the aquarium had long since cooled my rage at Knuckles Urbino's tone. Socks and underwear. The thought of walking around with wet feet and junk made me cringe, so I removed those, too, giving my fellow Silvers a decent look at it all.

Urbino's Number One Fan, the Silver called Parsons, eyed me up and down. "Shrinkage much?"

"I'm part Italian," I said. "I could hit you in the face with it from here if I wanted to."

Baxter laughed. Urbino said nothing and buzzed open the cage. I marched in. Things were about to get far colder and a hundred times more terrifying than I'd yet experienced in my brief employ here. There were grips for me to hold onto without worry of losing a hand to the beast's fangs. Naked, my panic barely reined in, I waited while Urbino closed the door with a punch of a button and sealed it with another. Then he activated the cable system and the cage rose off the platform. Cold air tickled me everywhere. Ten feet up, twenty, thirty—the crane swung and I levitated over the tank. Beneath, the thing I'd sensed studying all of us since our arrival performed a graceful spin away from the opposite side of the water and toward me.

I hung suspended over its head. Below me, the ominous shadow under the water waited. Urbino remained on the platform in control of my life. As he lowered me down into the tank, the others, I somehow knew, had taken action with military efficiency. They were at the other end of the platform, all now armed with what looked to be pool hoses and brushes with long handles. The cage dropped. My bare feet plunged into the frigid surf.

The ice bath wasn't the worst of it. That came when the living dinosaur from Loch Ness surged at the cage and threw its weight at the bars. The cage toppled. I gripped the supports with all my strength. Water splashed. Over that soundtrack, I heard the throaty predator's growl of the monster that sought to devour my flesh. Glacial, dark soup sprayed my face. The cage straightened and lowered even more, past my waist and then my stomach, up to my chest. *Shrinkage* would have been kind. I'd never done a polar plunge in January and had never wanted to. I imagined it felt something like this.

The cage dipped even deeper. Now, I was submerged to my throat. In that rising sense of panic, I wondered if Urbino would dunk me all the way—drown me for clocking him the previous night inside the secret interrogation chamber. But the cage stopped there. Eyes wide, teeth chattering, I waited.

Nestor circled close by, its mass creating waves. Holding onto the grips, I gazed at the frenzied surface of the water. Something large and terrifying lifted up from the murky stew. The head on that long serpent's neck turned my way. Nestor again growled. Breathing with the weight of the icy surf pressed against my chest was beyond painful, but on my next shallow sip of air, I smelled it. The monster from Loch Ness struck my nose like the damp underside of a log.

It studied me with alien eyes filled with a single emotion: hunger. Its mouth widening, I saw its teeth. And I saw them close up when its head lunged at the cage. Those sharp incisors connected with the bars. To my horror, I wasn't certain the protection would hold. The dinosaur's breath was feral, foul, and cold. I'd admitted awe of such a creature when I'd stood outside its tank in my black polo shirt with the stupid cartoon bat. Here, closer than I'd ever thought I'd get to it, I wished it had gone extinct with the rest of its kind.

Nestor released the bars and snapped at me again. Then the monster drew back and I sensed its mass in the surf just beyond the paltry and questionable safety offered by the cage. Once more, our gazes crossed. I fell into its black eyes, ravenous for me and, also, maybe trying to solve this puzzle that repeated every night but had yet to yield the human tidbit it sought to dine upon. My teeth clacked together, producing a mad music. I swore I'd never be warm again.

Another circle, and Nestor took off for the other end of the pool. The cage lifted up. I emerged from the brine, eyes stuck open, teeth playing a human xylophone. Across the tank, I saw Nestor in quick pursuit of something in the water, which it snatched up with sinister grace. A fish, I realized, but only because the monster tossed back its head like a seabird and gulped the catch down whole.

As soon as Nestor finished with that one morsel, it located another, and two more after that, swallowing them down with ease. I was shivering out of control and couldn't be certain, but I think I counted six catches, and I'm sure Nestor could have eaten ten times more that number.

The cage touched down on the platform. Urbino released the door. I stepped out and Parsons waited with a large, heated bath towel. He tossed it around me. Glorious warmth flooded back. My teeth ceased their chatter.

"Good work," Urbino offered. "This raises your previous score to a C."

I grunted and toweled off, pulled on my uniform, and we left for our next assignment.

En route to Frelling's Castle, I remembered my promise and asked to make a slight detour first. Urbino shot the idea down until

I mentioned that I'd made friends with the creature and anything that minimized threats to Silver Unit was a good thing, and so he caved. We jogged to my bungalow. I reminded them that they all knew the way, since they'd broken in for my abduction and official introduction to the baroness. This time, I had them wait outside and promised I'd only be a minute.

In one of the cardboard boxes, I located a paperback science fiction novel, a relic from my boyhood—*Moby Dick* by Herman Melville, and a mystery whose cover I couldn't remember ever cracking open. I tucked the mystery into one of the cargo pockets in my black uniform pants. The odor of Nestor's tank was still on me. More than anything, I wanted to shower. Instead, I returned to my four fellow soldiers and we jogged like cadets to Frelling's Castle.

Here the order was, at face value, simple. We were to feed and bathe the creature. Two of us would accomplish the latter duty while the others stripped and remade the bed with clean linens. Easy-peasy, right?

"Unless it doesn't want to be bathed," Urbino said.

"*He,*" I stressed.

Parsons sighed. "That's right, the two of you are besties now."

I shot him a look as we crossed the front lobby with its numerous Hollywood posters. "I just treated him with a little compassion. That goes a long way. You should try it some time."

Urbino unsealed the inner theater, home to my unexpected friend. The subdued lights over the stage shone down on the lone figure seated in a hunch on the bed. A curious mix of trepidation and melancholy gripped me. After the vampire queen and Nestor, I wasn't afraid, which was rather foolish of me, or so my inner critic warned. After all, I was defending a creature that hadn't been born like those surrounding me but one who'd been stitched together from multiple sources and the remains of many men.

Still, at that moment, it struck me that Frelling's Monster was my only real friend in the world.

He looked up and sighed, his face in a sour pout, his one good eye seeing us but looking through us. Urbino motioned for me to take point.

"Hey, buddy," I said.

Frelling's Monster returned to being present and recognized me despite my new attire. "Corey Lowen?"

"That's right," I said. "I promised I'd come back. Look—" I pulled the mystery novel out of my pocket. "I even brought something to read to you, like I promised."

I approached the stage and showed him the cover.

"*It was the start of a warm, gray autumn when a stranger approached the country home of the McCallister family seeking employment.* The butler did it," Frelling's Monster said. And then I opened to the first chapter to see he'd recited the opening sentence.

"Wow," I sighed. "You remember all that?"

"I've read this one before. And I remember *all*."

I stood there not knowing what to say. "I could pick up a romance novel, something new that you haven't read, like I originally offered."

"You kept your word. That's more important."

"Of course."

I sensed the others waiting to get started. *Screw them*, I thought.

"Buddy," I said. "You know the routine. They want me to help you get cleaned up. But you know what? I don't know your name."

"Frelling's Monster," he said.

I waved the dog-eared paperback at him. "No, your *real* name."

"The feet and one leg belong to a man named Holtzauer," the creature said. "The torso to a Mister Dunleavy. I never learned where the arms came from. The head…that was on the shoulders of Thomas Anderson before getting repositioned atop Dunleavy's neck. I'm all of them and none of them. So, you see, there is no real name."

"How about Buddy then?" I asked. "I mean, if we're gonna hang out together, I have to know what to call you. As my friend, I don't care much for Frelling's Monster, I have to say. You need a real name. No, you *deserve* one."

He studied me. Not sure why, I expected Frelling's Monster to cry. "Buddy?" he repeated in a voice not much louder than a whisper.

"Yeah, if you like it."

He nodded. "I do. I love it. *Buddy…*"

I tromped up the stairs to the stage and extended my hand. As the others watched, all as dumbfounded as my previous audience here, Buddy and I shook on it. "Now, how about we get you cleaned up? You can show me how it's usually done."

Buddy released my hand and pointed toward an alcove where a toilet and standup shower were located. "Usually, they have cattle prods."

"No need for that anymore, right?" I said and tipped an angry frown at Urbino and company. "Come on."

Buddy stood. Again, I was reminded of his height and ominous size—the strength possible in those altered muscles. But I felt no fear. Maybe I was still stunned from my unexpected swim in Nestor's tank. Being a Silver was like the training that Navy Seals experienced—meant to test prospective soldiers to their limitations. It was a great leap of faith, but I took it. We were friends.

I helped Buddy out of his clothes, which I discovered were held together with Velcro, and into the shower. His ankles remained cuffed.

"Don't worry, I had to strip down to feed Nestor about an hour ago," I said. "I'm all heart now when it comes to being naked in front of strangers."

"You and I aren't strangers," he said.

"That's right, pal."I turned on the shower and adjusted the water until it was reasonably hot.

"They never make it warm. It's always cold," Buddy said.

I absorbed that bit of intelligence and huffed out a swear. "Do you prefer it cold?"

"No."

"Okay, I've got it turned up. Tell me if it's too hot."

He stepped in, moaned. "It's ideal, Corey."

"Good. You don't ever have to shower cold again."

I reached for the large square of soap and handed it to him. Buddy lathered up, rinsed off. Behind me, my fellow Silvers stripped the bedclothes and prepared his dinner.

"You said you remember well, Buddy. That was pretty impressive, you reciting the opening page of the novel."

He soaped up his hair, which stood in lathered spikes and should have appeared funny. Anywhere and on anyone else, it would have. "I can recite verbatim everything I've ever read or had read to me."

I considered that revelation. "Does anyone know that you're a genius?"

Buddy shrugged. "You're the first person who's bothered to ask me."

I shook my head. He rinsed his hair. I pulled a clean towel off the shelf and handed it to him, doing my best to not stare at his many scars as he dried himself.

"I won't hurt you, Corey," he said suddenly.

"I know, Buddy. We've got each other's backs."

I located a fresh change of clothes on the same shelf, more of those black hospital scrubs with Velcro. While helping Buddy into them, he leaned closer. His breath smelled sour, and it dawned on me that not only had we failed to brush his teeth, but they hadn't provided any of the expected tools to perform that duty.

"Corey," he whispered in a voice meant only for me. "Be wary of those who are in charge of this place. Ravi Nakur and those above him."

"The council?" I asked.

Buddy nodded. "The Council of Georges who run Monsterland. They're the true monsters!" He drew back. We finished dressing him.

My expression must have betrayed my surprise after we returned to the stage that was his home and prison, because Parsons commented. "See something in there that made you jealous, Lowen?"

"Yeah, your father's junk," I retorted.

They'd placed a tray on a folding table beside the bed. On it were various slops and mashes that looked like the equivalent of hospital food. "What the hell is this?" I asked.

"The proper nutrition for your good friend," Urbino answered from the edge of the stage, beyond Buddy's reach.

Buddy sat and started to eat. I remained standing beside him in a defensive posture. "Wait—is that what they feed you every night?"

Buddy nodded and grunted around the spoon in his mouth.

"Tomorrow night, I'll bring you something better. Anything you want. Just name it."

Buddy looked up, his expression that of a hopeful kid. "I heard the famous Monsterland grilled cheese sandwiches are pretty good."

"We saved the best for last," Urbino said.

"Oh, yeah," Baxter chuckled.

The hours had passed slowly and I was feeling them along with the physical stress of the job. At some point during the jog from Frelling's Castle to the haunted house where the queen of the vampires and her brood were kept, I wondered about the longevity of such a job. Being part of Silver Unit was, I mused, like a career in pro football—how long could a man maintain his sturdiness before concussions took their toll? Or adult entertainment, when the demands of performing again and again shriveled a man's scrotum into something that resembled a discolored, brown iguana clamped between his legs?

We entered through the private security door. I found myself in a mirrored room where multitudes of Knuckles Urbinos, Baxters, Parsonses, Corey Lowens, and others reflected on and on into eternity.

"One more protection against the baroness and her gang of far-out thugs," Urbino said.

"Because they can't see their reflections?" I asked.

"That's not exactly how it works. They *can* see a kind of reflection, but it hurts them to face it directly. Tends to be too hideous for them to handle. There's a theory that in Greek mythology; Medusa and the rest of the Gorgons were really vampires. That whole turning-to-stone thing was her freezing her victims through hypnosis."

Parsons located a door hidden among the mirrors. Beyond it was another mirrored corridor. That led to a room with an upright refrigerator and a window above one of those slide-through slots you see in prison cells to feed the convicted. The small anteroom was similarly mirrored.

"Do the honors, Parsons," Urbino commanded.

"Yes sir!"

Parsons moved to the refrigerator and opened it. Inside were intravenous bags in plastic, only they contained blood instead of saline solution. I wondered which ones were full of swine hemoglobin.

"You'll notice the safeguards," Urbino said to me.

I did. Above the mirrored walls, the ceiling sported a network of pipes.

"Loaded with silver solution and garlic?" I asked.

Urbino nodded. "Enough to melt them all the instant one of those bloodsucking freaks tries to wiggle through the slot on a wisp of fog. We don't screw around with vampires."

"I guess not," I said.

Parsons rapped on the closed tray with his knuckles. Something on the other side knocked back. He opened the slot and extended five bags of human red blood cells through. Greedy hands adorned with jeweled rings grabbed at them. Urbino waved me over to the window and rolled back the metal covering.

On the other side was a view into the vampires' groovy pad. Baroness von Ullmer raised a martini glass filed with O-Negative or A-Positive, a sharp little smirk displayed on that gorgeous face.

"Cheers," she said, her voice reaching past the slot.

The others, her male acolytes and the one female vampress with blonde bangs and beauty mark, held similar glasses for a toast. Music played behind them, something British, classic, barely audible but just enough that I envied them, all dressed so smartly and seeming to enjoy themselves. Life behind the mirrors was one big party. If not for the choice of cocktails or the way the baroness and her brood slurped them down, I might have liked to join them.

The baroness lowered her martini glass, now drained of all but the barest of corpuscles. As I watched, she licked up the dregs, set her glass down, and, tossing back her mane, she broke into a spirited dance straight out of the 1960s. The others all followed suit, gyrating in place as though in some kind of epileptic fit. The moves were something from the past but, for a moment, it seemed the baroness was waiting for me to follow them in dance from my side of the window. Heaven help me, I would have done it if not for the audience, the mirrors, and that toothy, bloody grin she flashed my way.

The sun was up when we exited the vampire house. A bite infused the morning air, a reminder that spring was young and winter not far behind us, but after my experience in Nestor's tank, I figured I could handle January dressed in only my underwear, no sweat.

Urbino had us jog around the park perimeter. I was thinking we were done for the night—we'd certainly done enough—when he directed us back to the giant fish tank containing the remains of the Great Lakester.

"Checkpoint Zero," Urbino said. "This is where the night always starts and ends."

I was tired, my nerves frayed. We shook out our arms and legs near the place where the giant's head rested in death. Though gone for years, I expected those eyes to blink, that mouth to snap at us, the monster awakened from hibernation by the movements of our nearby bodies. I wanted a shower. I longed to sleep. The day warmed around us in the deceptive silence of the park.

"So, we done here?" I asked.

"Not yet," Urbino said.

He and Parsons exchanged a look. None of the other two said anything. My skin prickled.

"Is this some joke or secret that everyone else knows except me?" I asked, punctuating the question with a tired laugh.

"No joke," Urbino said. "This way."

He led us around to the foot of the structure where another security door not accessible to the public was secreted among the aquarium's sturdy supports. My exhausted brain wondered if this was a way into the actual tank. Urbino used his ID to open the door and I discovered the access led *beneath* it.

We descended metal steps, me behind Parsons and ahead of Baxter and Roman, the other two Silvers.

"Watch your head," Urbino warned.

The tips of my hair brushed the roof of a small, oblong room located beneath the lake monster's tank. Energy pulsed through the air—what felt identical to the Hum. Up close, the protection of my uniform couldn't completely ward it off. The room's only features were a door—metal, sealed, with plenty of rivets and a sign that proclaimed, simply **DANGER!** on it, and a workstation with various meters and gauges and a metal chair.

"You might have wondered about what would happen if we ever suffered a power failure," Urbino said. I realized he was talking to me. "This is the biggest and best of our safeguards. It guarantees that the juice will always flow and we'll never have to worry about an interruption or escaping monsters."

He gripped his ID and approached the door.

"No one goes in there but me," he said. "Turn around."

The others followed the order. I caught Urbino's leer and did as instructed. I heard the door unlock and swing open and, for only a second before it again sealed behind Knuckles Urbino, I caught the flash of indigo light on the metal wall I faced.

Indigo—the source of the energy Urbino referenced…it was the Abyss! That's where it was kept, in a secret room beneath the Great Lakester!

Seconds swelled and dragged on. Eventually, the door opened and footsteps sounded at my back.

"You can turn around now," Urbino said. "Everything's operating in the green."

The indigo, *you mean,* my inner jokester snarked. I turned around. Urbino's expression wasn't as cocky or cool as it had been throughout the long night. *Of course not—he's just taken an audience with the Abyss!*

"Fall out," he ordered.

I translated that into vacating the secret room. I trudged up the stairs behind Roman and whacked my head on the metal roof. Baxter snickered behind me. I didn't hold it against him. After all, Urbino had warned me of the danger.

I walked back to my bungalow—I'd done enough jogging for one night. A few bodies in khaki pants and black polo shirts were out and about. The night shift was done. The day belonged to oblivious Monsterlanders who would never risk setting foot inside the sasquatch enclosure or be submerged up to their bare throats with Nestor.

Dark thoughts plagued me as I ambled through the pleasant temperature and morning glare. The Council of Georges? Buddy's warning unnerved me nearly as much as the revelation that the Abyss was housed in secret beneath the giant fish tank containing the preserved corpse of the Great Lakester. My mind felt almost as depleted of energy as my legs, but I trusted Buddy and his claim about Ravi Nakur—the way he'd stopped my fist in mid-punch…even before that, the man had triggered all of my warning flags.

The Council of Georges. What an odd name for shareholders. Even thinking it unleashed a shiver down my spine. Was it because they were all named George? "Stupid," I blurted out on the last leg of my walk to the bungalow.

Again, I strutted past the bamboo, backtracked, and found the path leading up to my front door. Monsterland was full of secret places and passages. None of us was told the absolute truth by those in charge. All of the money and perks tossed my way didn't seem to equal the amount of jeopardy I now faced. The world had been so much saner when the monsters were still lurking under beds, not put on display at Monsterland.

I passed Bungalow Two and inserted my key card into my lock. As the lock released, the door to II opened, and a man exited. Older, he was dressed in a fine suit of maybe Italian design and cut that cost thousands. His silver hair's style probably set him back a small fortune as well. He wore a casual expression on his face and a gold ring with a fat onyx stone on his right hand. That ring looked old, priceless.

He regarded me, a bedraggled skilled worker in a black military uniform, with a curt nod. My neighbor had been engaged in sweaty abandon with a lady friend on the night Knuckles Urbino and company shanghaied me to my meeting with the baroness. No words were exchanged. I wondered if he was one of the Georges.

In the shower, the shakes began. I cranked the dial up to scalding. The cold had wormed deeper inside me than could be reached. I willed the tremors to steady. They did. But very clearly, I saw myself suffering a kind of post-traumatic shock at the end of every shift. An echo of the Hum, maybe, which I now guessed originated from the thing imprisoned beneath the dead lake monster's gigantic corpse.

Leaning with my face into the spray, I mentally shuffled through Monsterland's attractions. Buddy wasn't a true monster but a sad innocent. The mummies only wanted to sleep, and I could cut them plenty of slack—the evil glances they shot at spectators were the result of constantly being zapped awake against their will. When you thought it through, Nestor wasn't any more evil than a great white shark or killer whale. And as for the baroness and her fellow party animals, they didn't strike me as being necessarily *evil* even though they'd committed numerous deeds that could be counted as such. No, they were throwbacks to another era that liked to dance and drink and hang upside down from the rafters like bats when the sun was up. I could even be merciful to the sasquatch family despite their dietary preferences.

But the Abyss was different.

A monster from the stars, according to the baroness. Malevolence radiated from it. And just as evil was the sense I got when I thought about those in charge of this seemingly family-friendly tourist destination they'd built. As Buddy had warned me, Ravi and the Council of Georges were the true monsters of Monsterland.

Boom.

Distant thunder rocked the world. I roused from my thoughts and drew down my gaze from the sky, which had suddenly grown overcast.

Boom.

The thunder echoed around me. To my surprise, it hadn't originated in the sky but came from beneath my sneakers.

Boom.

I gazed back up. Looming at the tops of the surrounding trees were the upper tracks of the Dragon Express. Beyond it—and striding closer—came the giant monster from Lake Erie, its booming footsteps the cause of the tremors and vibrations.

Ice formed instantly in my bowels. I froze. The roller coaster proved to be no impediment to the colossus, any more than the concrete and steel buildings of Cleveland had been on that rainy day in the past. The Great Lakester let out a deafening roar and smashed through a length of tall track. Metal and wood rained down. It was like I was seeing the destruction of a child's toy rather than an engineered iron structure. The horror bellowed again with its giant head tossed back.

Run, my inner voice urged. But my feet had transformed into cement. I stood there immobile. The Great Lakester surged forward and hurled its mass through what remained of the Dragon Express. The ground quaked. My leg muscles woke. My feet unstuck.

As I turned, I risked another glance up, and I saw that the horror's eyes glowed indigo. Only a nightmare, that's all this was. The Abyss was screwing with me again.

"Wake up," I blathered, my lips flaccid from sleep.

The monster strode forward. Its indigo gaze located me on the ground. It leaned down and roared. My ears popped from the sound blast. The last of my paralysis broke. I ran—

And ran.

At my back, trees toppled and buildings were flattened. In the insanity of my attempt to escape, I wondered if a giant's footfalls could crush mummies. I mean, stomp them flat enough to remove the curse that kept them imprisoned in their current, half-life state. Fake pyramids would be no obstacles to a beast as powerful as the one pursuing me.

Neither would a hundred and ninety pounds of skin, flesh, and bone.

"You can't escape me," that hideous child's voice tittered at my back. "You *hurt* me when you grabbed hold."

"I'm sorry."

"No, you're not!"

"You're right about that. I'm not sorry I unleashed the pain."

"And I intend to hurt you!"

I dug in my soles, halted, and turned around. The Lake Monster was gone. When I spun back, I was greeted by a version of Knuckles Urbino, one with glowing indigo eyes.

We faced off against one another.

"Nice scar," I said.

"Oh, you mean *this*?" The Urbino-thing that wasn't Urbino reached both hands up to its mangled cheek, dug at and tore open skin, and pulled. Instead of blood, sparkles of indigo light oozed out and dripped down my adversary's borrowed face.

"Disgusting," I said defiantly.

Urbino-thing ceased burrowing and eyed me with surprise. "You think I'm disgusting? Imagine what I must see when I look upon you primitive abominations!"

"Oh? You sound awfully high and mighty."

Urbino-thing smiled. Indigo light flashed behind its teeth. "You have no idea."

"Enlighten me."

"Compared to me, you are single-celled organisms, weak and pathetic. You want to know who I am?"

I motioned with my right hand—*blah, blah, blah.*

Urbino-thing's grin tightened. "I am the center of terror. I am all the devils in all of your world's mythologies. I am the Abyss. I am…"

He leaned in, and my flesh reacted by flash freezing. My stomach soured. My nostrils crinkled. A shadow stained my vision.

"…*God,*" it whispered, laughing in that sinister falsetto.

I woke facedown on my bed in a puddle of drool and tears.

Sunlight spilled down from blue sky. I looked at the clock on my phone. It was only three in the afternoon. Invisible ice lay over my skin and refused to thaw. I finished a second cup of coffee from the maker in the bungalow's kitchenette and waited for the robust blend to kick into gear. When it failed to warm me, I paced some more. The Abyss was inside my head. It was stalking me. It knew who I was. The baroness was correct in her claim that the nightmares would get worse.

I'd ask her to remove the memory. Sure, that would solve it. But when would I be given such an opportunity without an audience? And if *that* audience were present, news would reach Ravi pretty damn fast that I *had* managed to grasp hold of the Abyss, however briefly, and, according to the baroness, that would be my certain doom.

I dressed in fresh jeans and a clean shirt that smelled of Linda's laundry soap, pocketed my keys and wallet, and locked the bungalow's front door behind me. I followed the path to the Human Resources building and continued past it into the park. I rounded the mummy exhibit which shined in the sunlight like a counterfeit version of the Valley of Kings in Egypt.

It struck me that, yes, I'd become one of those people who live for their jobs. Literally, I was *living* at my job. During my time off, here I was, walking through the same park by day that I jogged at night. The cacophony of the crowd's excited, combined voices, played in the background behind my thoughts. The Abyss. The Georges. Buddy.

My pal, Buddy.

I diverted from my aimless amble across the thoroughfare to the Transylvanian Café. There, I ordered two Monster Cheese sammies, an equal number of soups to go, and a pair of their giant turtle brownies—Black Magic Brownies according to the menu. The food arrived in a colorful takeout bag bearing the park's cartoon bat logo. I'd promised Buddy something other than slop for tonight's dinner and planned to follow through.

Outside once more, I donned my shades. The intention was to return to my bungalow and grab some more sleep—hopefully without dreams—in readiness for another grueling night shift.

"Smith?" a man's voice called.

G.I. Bo strutted up to me, clad in khakis and black polo shirt uniform. "I thought it was you!"

I wasn't sure why, but after the company of Urbino, Baxter, Parsons, and Roman, I was grateful to be around someone whose motives I could define clearly. "Yeah, it's me. Least I think so."

I extended my hand, knowing it was a mistake. Bo shook it hard enough to make me wince.

"Jesus, would you lighten up a bit?" I said. "And my name's not Smith."

Bo chuckled but made no apology. "I won't, and I know that. Cope."

We sat on a bench in the shade not far from the nightmare merry-go-round.

"Care to share?" he asked, indicating the bag of takeout.

"No," I said.

"So what's it like?" he asked. "The night shift?"

I gazed across the vista at all those unsuspecting people who had no real clue as to what happened behind the scenes—the dangers and secrets and truths that went into the bands around their wrists and the cotton candy they ate between attractions.

"It's work," I said.

"You lucky bastard," Bo grumbled.

"Lucky?"

He nodded. "You think I signed onto this place to stack coffee mugs in the gift shop or take tickets at the front gate? No, *amigo*—I expected to do the actual heavy lifting. You know, the shit you're doing after hours. The *real* job. Monsters and making sure they stay put right where they are."

"There's a lot more to it than patriotism," I sighed. "There's grunt work—and it's dangerous."

"I've done grunt work. *Dangerous* grunt work," Bo said. "Why couldn't I have been the one to get assigned trash duty the day that foreign agent broke into the park in a dumpster?"

I looked at the bag of takeout on the bench beside me. "You might have been a bit heavy-handed with Buddy."

"Buddy?"

"Frelling's Creature," I said.

"You mean your pal, the monster?"

I shook my head. "He isn't a monster, Bo. Dude's got more brains than anyone I know."

"That's because Doctor Frelling probably dumped more than one brain in his skull!"

"See, that's where you're wrong. You and everyone else. He isn't a monster anymore than you or I are."

"Fine. I'll make friends with him—if you put in a good word for me with Ravi."

I studied Bo through narrowed eyes. "Huh?"

"Yeah, Ravi likes you. Trusts you. You're his golden boy," Bo said. "If you put in a word for me, I'm sure he'll listen. That way I could be part of Silver Unit, too. I already got my military background—"

"I don't know."

"Be a friend, like you are to that monster. Help me out."

I remembered my own brother's lack of support when it came to a job at the hospital where Vinnie worked security. Without intending to, Bo had socked me where I was vulnerable. "Maybe."

"You will. I believe in you, dude."

"I'll see what I can do," I said. "No promises."

G.I. Bo stood and adjusted himself without embarrassment. "I'll be a plus, you'll see. Especially after they caught that intruder, for sure."

As I processed his words, Bo hawked up a wad of phlegm and spat it onto the shady pavement. "What did you say?" I asked.

"You didn't hear?" he laughed. "Figured you mucky-mucks in Silver Unit would be the first to know. They caught her on the roller coaster this morning hiding in one of the cars. She still had on your uniform shirt!"

I entered Human Resources and approached the receptionist.

"Mister Lowen," the familiar girl in khakis and black polo shirt, the chubby one with dark hair, greeted me sunnily from the other side of the desk.

"I need to see Ravi."

"Mister Nakur's unavailable," she answered in a cheery voice. She was so damn polite and happy. Too much so. "Would you like to leave a message for him?"

"I'll wait."

I returned to that line of miserable chairs, the same ones from conference rooms and doctors' offices elsewhere in the park. I picked up a glossy industry magazine—*Visitor's Choice*—and flipped through pages. Inside were fluffy, puffy articles about destinations like the glass walking platform at the Grand Canyon and recreated rain forests ideal for today's upscale, urban adventurers. The phone rang at the reception desk. She answered.

"No, that would be a different extension. Let me transfer you to Lost and Found. One moment."

I crossed a leg over the other in an attempt to appear jaunty. The bright colors in the pages before me blurred. You wouldn't find any articles about the Abyss inside *Visitor's Choice*. Did every theme park or tourist destination have its own version of the Council of Georges? I exhaled a sigh through my nostrils. What did I plan to ask Ravi apart from an update on my attacker with the zap stick? It struck me that my anger was misdirected, part of my growing mistrust of those in charge inflamed by my knowledge of facts I wasn't supposed to have learned.

"Your food's gonna get cold," the receptionist said.

I peered over the top of the magazine at her. She was all smiles, and I wondered if Ravi had gotten the baroness to do some kind of whammy on her—*forget your troubles, be happy, so very god-damned happy!*

I tipped a glance at the bag of takeout. "You're right." I returned the magazine to the top of the miserable torture device chair next to the one my ass was plunked upon, picked up my takeout, and stood.

"Do you want me to leave a message for Mister Nakur?" she asked sweetly.

"No, I'm good," I lied. Then, flashing my own lunatic's smile, I exited the building and wandered behind to the walkway, the bamboo and fucked-up design where paths vanished and reappeared in a sort of confused reality.

At 11:45 I walked to the dead giant's glass coffin where my fellow Silvers had gathered.

"You know the drill," Urbino said.

We again began with the sasquatches, whose funky stink was almost too thick to breathe. I scooped up their shit and we left them mushrooms. We hastened out of their prison. Again, Uncle Lou made a grab at me, but I was ready this time, so he didn't get nearly as close.

We raked the sand in the mummy enclosure. Given my own troubles with sleep lately, I appreciated their predicament more. The ones pushing the power button, keeping them in constant motion during the day, were their version of the Abyss. I intentionally raked slower to allow them a few extra Zs.

"Lowen—*hustle*," Knuckles Urbino snapped.

Oh well, I tried.

At the Loch Ness aquarium, I removed a boot. Parsons chortled.

"That one's eager," Urbino said. "But you can cancel the striptease for tonight, Lowen."

Parsons clapped me on the back and walked out of sight. I'd mentally prepared to go into the tank, but that wasn't the plan.

"Not today," Urbino said. "You're with the others on cleanup and feeding duty."

I followed Baxter and Roman to a maintenance locker where the long brushes and pool vacuum were stored. An anteroom in the same wing off the platform contained a lesser aquarium, inside which large fish swam. Salmon, I suspected.

"We have to scrub down the walls of the tank," Roman said. "And suck up the sludge."

"Sludge?"

"Also known as Loch Ness Monster shit."

"Oh."

It wasn't rocket science. We just had to be careful. Parsons was the decoy this time. When I emerged back onto the platform, Nestor's dark mass was already in motion beneath the water, Parsons stood in the shark cage. Not lost on me was the fact that my fellow Silver had stripped out of his black uniform and changed into a wetsuit, which I figured was far warmer an option than decoying Nestor in one's birthday suit.

They'd sure had their fun with me.

"Everyone takes his turn in the cage," Roman said. "Make it fast. We don't want Nestor losing interest in the bait and making a grab at us while we're leaning over the pool."

Corey Lowen, pool boy, I thought as I scrubbed and then vacuumed.

We did what was expected. Baxter wheeled out a cart that contained half a dozen struggling salmon in buckets and dumped them over the edge of the pool. Urbino pulled Parsons out of the drink, then Nestor fed.

I snuck back to my place long enough to nuke the grilled cheese Monsters and soup and rejoined the others at Frelling's Castle.

"What the hell is that?" Urbino demanded.

"Dinner for my friend."

He shook his head. "It's against the rules. That thing eats what they tell us to feed it, nothing else."

I faced off against my new supervisor the same way I had in a recent nightmare and mostly didn't back down. But I remembered the gouging of his scar in the dream and the indigo-colored blood that had seeped out and almost blinked first.

"Please," I said. "Would you want to eat that same slop night after night?"

"We don't know if he can handle real food."

I laughed. "Thousands of people a day handle that food. Besides, think of the benefits to this unit."

"Benefits?"

"My buddy in there—" I tipped my chin at the stage behind the doors. "He's so much more agreeable when you let me take point."

"Lowen's correct," another man's voice said.

I turned to see that Ravi had entered the lobby, having done so with the stealth of a skilled predator. Also, that he now wore the black uniform of Silver Unit and it fit him with easy perfection.

"He is?" Urbino questioned.

Ravi eyed me. For the first time, I truly saw him as the dangerous man he was. Maybe it was the uniform or what I knew in secret about him, the warnings from not one but two of Monsterland's headlining attractions. Perhaps it was all that and something more. The Abyss.

"Our Mister Lowen has neutralized a tangible threat—the Monster's rage—by appealing to its soul even though it doesn't have one. What's a little variation in diet compared to that?"

Urbino huffed, "You heard the boss."

Ravi strutted over. I'd wanted to clock him that night with the baroness. I wanted to again now but realized it was fruitless anger. Ravi Nakur was a trained soldier despite his floppy mop of hair and willowy physique.

"You wanted to see me earlier in the day, Lowen," he said. "Here I am."

My mouth suddenly dry, I explained myself. "Yeah, it was about me bringing Buddy something other than the usual gruel."

"Buddy?" Ravi asked.

"Frelling's Creature. I wanted to go through proper channels. That, and I heard you nabbed the intruder."

Ravi maintained his spare smile. "It's good to respect the chain of command. You already have my permission to feed the monster…*Buddy*…a different dinner tonight. As for the intruder, the situation's been dealt with."

"Do we know who she is, why she did it?" I pressed.

My question removed Ravi's smile. "Just another zealot without a cause. This isn't the first time we've had political extremists attempt to make a statement here. Sadly, I doubt it will be the last. You go ahead, do your job with your new friend Buddy. I'd like to speak to Mister Urbino alone."

I didn't linger. I entered the theater where Parsons, Baxter, and Roman waited.

Buddy noticed me and stood. "Corey Lowen," he said.

I waved the bag of takeout. "Hey, Buddy I got you one of those Monster Grilled Cheese sandwiches, soup, and dessert. And I made it a double order."

Buddy looked perplexed. "What if I can't finish both?"

I chuckled. "That second order isn't for you, dude—that's mine. You didn't think I was gonna make you eat alone, did you?"

I helped him wash and dress, then we returned to the bed with its clean change of sheets. I opened the takeout bag. The food had gone lukewarm in the meanwhile, but I figured it was still far better than the mashes and slop my friend normally choked down at chow time.

"May I?" I asked, indicating the corner of empty cot.

Buddy eyed me. "Of course."

I sat. Then I handed him the food along with a plastic soup spoon, which was hardly anything that could be weaponized, and a handful of brown napkins made from recycled paper. Nervousness radiated off my new friend. Without addressing his worry, I ripped open the lid of my container, pulled out half my sandwich, and ate.

"I haven't tried the turtle brownie yet," I said between bites. "They say they're filled with black magic, but I doubt that's part of the recipe. They look pretty friggin' awesome, though."

Buddy hesitated. "Turtle brownies? Are they made from real turtles?"His expression was serious.

"No, they're not," I said, only to catch his smile. I laughed. "Okay, you had me there. Good one."

Buddy lifted half of his sandwich and tested it with his nose before taking a tentative bite. His one good eye rolled in its socket. The other would have had it been aligned properly.

"You like?" I asked.

Buddy's good eye misted over. "Thank you," he said in a voice barely louder than a whisper.

I waved my free hand. "Ain't no thing."

"No, it's *everything*, Corey," he said.

I lifted the lid from my soup. It had gone tepid, too, and somewhat gloppy, but it tasted good. "Any time. I got permission from the Big Cheese himself."

"Ravi Nakur?" Buddy asked, suddenly wary.

In a lower voice, I said, "It's okay. Eat up before it gets cold. Or colder."

We ate. How we got on the subject of my brother, I wasn't exactly sure. "He was my dad's favorite. I was more of an outsider, an observer. It's old news now, but it still, you know, stings."I left out the part about that morning when the room shook and my father's beer bottle exploded and all the blood from his cut hand.

"My father stitched my arms on without any anesthesia," Buddy said.

"*Touché*, you win the contest."

"Does your brother know how you feel?"

I shrugged. "He must."

"Tell him."

I exhaled through my nostrils. "It's probably too late. We recently left things on a fairly sour note."

"If it bothers you, you should fix it."

I flashed a weak grin at him. "Thanks."

And then it struck me—I was getting solid relationship advice on family matters from Frelling's Creature, who most people thought was a monster. I faced him. A smear of chocolate from a turtle brownie stained one corner of his mouth.

"You're okay, Buddy."

"So are you, Corey."

I extended my right hand, knuckles aimed at him. He balled his gigantic hand into a fist, and we knocked knuckles together.

"Can we do this again?" Buddy asked.

"Sure thing."

"Maybe…?" he started.

I waited for him to finish the sentence. "Go on," I eventually urged.

"I'd love to see what's out there."

I tracked his focus past the stadium seating to the open doors leading to the lobby. "There? It's just a stupid hallway with some posters of *Frankenstein* and a shitty portrait of Doctor Frelling."

"No, I meant beyond. Outside."

"You mean the park?" He nodded. "I don't know about that. I don't think they'd let me…"

Frowning, he turned away. Guilt stabbed at my heart.

"But I'll ask. A field trip, sure."

"Thank you, Corey. You're a great friend. Your brother is lucky to have you."

"So I keep telling him."

"Tell him again."

I promised I would. I made Buddy wipe his mouth, gathered up the empty containers and wrappers, and extended my hand once more. We shook.

"Be good," I said and then wandered off the stage, aware that Buddy's eyes tracked me the entire way like those of a loyal dog.

Ravi and the others waited in the lobby. Our boss stood with his arms folded and that same constipated smirk on his face. "Impressive," Ravi said.

"Why? Because you just realized he's an actual person?"

"It's a bunch of spare parts. No, what's impressive is that you're so comfortable around it. *Him*, if you prefer," he corrected before I could make him. "It takes all of Silver Unit to bathe and feed Frelling's Monster, yet you accomplish it by yourself."

"Maybe rethink your approach. Lose the cattle prods and the attitudes. I treat him with respect, like an equal."

"I see that."

"How about you let me take him outside some night. Let him get some fresh air, stretch his legs."

Ravi laughed, the outburst short, sharp, cold. "Oh, that will never happen."

"Why not?"

"The dangers, the threat—*the insurance risk,*" Ravi stressed. "A grilled cheese is one thing. A stroll through the park entirely something else."

I chose my next words carefully. "You hired me to do a job. I'm trying to do it."

"Then do as you're instructed," Ravi said. "Anything else to say?"

"Only that if you're open to the idea, and you want more muscle at night, you should consider promoting Bo Wolcotte to Silver Unit."

Ravi laughed again. "Wolcotte? Are you joking?"

"He's ex-military, and he's eager."

"He'd be dead before the end of his first shift," Ravi said gravely. "Wolcotte's operating on fewer brain cells than your other friend in there." He tipped his chin at the theater doors.

We all are, I thought. And oh, how I wanted to illuminate Ravi that Buddy was a genius, a man of words and books. But it was a wasted effort to even try. More so, one fraught with jeopardy. The man in that black uniform was an assassin. Wiser to not let him think I knew how dangerous he was.

"You got anything else for the supervisor, Lowen?" Urbino asked.

I shook the takeout bag filled with empty containers and dirty napkins. "Just that I'll dispose of this properly when we pass the next trash barrel, *Master*."

Yes, best to let Ravi Nakur think I was an obedient peon in the Monsterland food chain.

We approached the security entrance at the rear of the vampire house. Urbino released the door. Not sure why, a shiver teased the nape of my neck, which was sweaty from our synchronized jog to reach the night's penultimate stop. I tried to ignore it, knowing that was foolish. Every sense of wrongness in this place was to be trusted and heeded.

We entered the room of mirrors. Urbino had Parsons attend to gathering the blood bags. "Make it six," he said.

"Six?" Parsons questioned, only to receive a look from our boss. "Yes, sir."

"The baroness has earned an extra round," Urbino said. Like the warning of the shiver, I knew he was lying.

Roman opened the meal slot and Parsons distributed the blood bags. Standing there, I eyed the view beyond the glass. There was the baroness, dressed in an ethereal number cut low on the bottom, her shapely legs in white tights, a vision of beauty from another era. And there were her minions, the men clad in Nehru jackets and rock-and-roll striped pants, the other women in romper and cat suit. At first, I was so bewitched by Ursula von Ullmer's otherworldly radiance that the math eluded me.

Baroness von Ullmer. Her three male consorts. Her two female besties. There should have been five total. So why did the headcount add up to *six*?

The chill returned. I stared past the glass at the small crowd on the other side as they emptied the contents of the blood bags into their martini glasses and toasted us before slurping down the thick, cold contents. Eyes wide, I broke focus with the baroness, trained my gaze past the males, and regarded each of the two females, one at a time. I remembered the blonde with the bangs and birthmark. The brunette, second female vampire hungrily lapping at the inside of her martini glass, wasn't familiar. At least not as far as my previous visits to this groovy destination.

But as I stared into the exhibit, and the chill teasing my neck somersaulted down my spine, I thought I recognized her from our brief encounter long days earlier. My lower jaw dropped as a swear charged past my lips before I could trap it.

"Something wrong, Lowen?" Urbino asked.

I blinked myself out of the trance and got back into character. "No, sir, just in awe watching the show."

"Close it up," Urbino ordered.

The meal slot clanged shut and got secured, the room again sealed up against escape. We resumed our jog in the direction of the night's final stop—the secret underground bunker beneath the Great Lakester where the Abyss was imprisoned.

Back in the cool night air, my entire body tingled with an unpleasant itch. That sixth vampire…somehow, I knew she was the intruder who'd zapped me at the dumpsters. And I knew that Ravi had seen to her murder. Worse, to her eternal sentence as one of the undead inside his theme park of monsters.

The food in my gut burbled. I wanted to puke. I almost did when we descended into the secret chamber beneath the aquarium and the Hum worked past my uniform's defenses.

Back in my bungalow, I ran the cold water in the kitchenette sink and plunged my head beneath the stream. I felt hot and twitchy all over. The water worked its magic. I closed my eyes and tried to think.

Murder, my inner voice shrieked.

I shot up, my head soaked, my stomach in chaos. The sour lemon warning that I was about to hurl filled my mouth. I made it to the bathroom and chucked up everything that was and wasn't in my stomach. Thick tears clotted in my eyes. I puked again. My guts lurched a third time, but I kept whatever was left down. Depleted, I flushed the toilet, rinsed my mouth, and brushed my teeth. After spitting out the toothpaste suds, I fixated on the image of the toothbrush whose handle boasted a tiny cartoon bat. It was only one small element of the numerous perks I'd been granted since taking the job, a bonus from Monsterland, Ravi Nakur, and the Council of Georges who ran things from the shadows. Seeing the toothbrush twisted my guts all over again into hurling, even if there was nothing left to ralph up.

I was an accessory to their crime. I hadn't done the deed, but in working for them, I bore a measure of guilt. Whoever she was, she was dead now, reanimated through the vampire's curse, and I had played a part in the sequence of events which led to this morning and its ugly truths. No trial. No sentence to jail. An eternity in hell.

Using my pointer finger for a toothbrush, I scrubbed again, which was ridiculous—the toothpaste, like the brush with the bat, was part of the bonus I'd received. My *blood* bonus—literally! I could ignore the toothbrush and toothpaste, but what about the water I used to rinse the foul taste from my mouth? The bed calling to me to curl atop it in a fetal position and sleep? Everything but the contents of a few garbage bags and cardboard cartons I possessed I owed to Monsterland.

I was a monster now.

I gargled with blood bonus mouthwash, showered with blood bonus soap and high-end shampoo, then crawled into my blood bonus bed. I wanted to hate her, that sixth vampire and former freedom fighter—hate her for breaking into the park and putting me into this position. If G.I. Bo had been on trash duty like he lamented, I'd still be on day shift with my fellow green Monsterlanders, taking tickets and performing other mundane, murder-less tasks. I'd maybe date Martine. Not that I had much to offer other than a genuine heart and, until tonight, a soul mostly unblemished apart from making one room shake in my father's old house. I'd still be holed up in Vinnie's and Linda's basement rec room. I'd be in Limbo rather than Hell.

I tossed onto my left side and closed my eyes.

They shot open a second later.

Buddy had been correct about Ravi and the council. So, too, had the baroness in her warning to not reveal that I'd shown some measure of dominance over the Abyss, even with my mental switch stuck in the halfway position. Ravi Nakur was dangerous, a murderer. I could go to the authorities, tell them what I knew. A whistleblower, sure—but would they believe me? And once word got back that I'd ratted him out, what would Ravi do?

Oh, that answer was clear enough—retribution. The payback for my loose tongue would be stiff and absolute. I'd either find myself grooving to the oldies alongside the intruder-turned-vampire in the baroness's coven, or Urbino's men and my replacement would be vacuuming my digested remains out of Nestor's swimming pool. *Keep your cool. Don't show any sign that you know the truth. The truth about how shady and shitty they are. That the real monsters are the ones in charge.* My inner voice warned me to lay low until I figured out what to do. And I listened to that advice. By day, I slept and suffered increasingly terrifying nightmares about the Abyss. By night, I chucked mushrooms and scooped up sasquatch scat and, when it was my turn in the rotation, entered the shark cage—in a wetsuit.

April slipped into May. The days, most spent within the fortress walls of Monsterland, lost cohesion and blurred together. I'd escaped the rec room, had a burgeoning bank account, and at least one legit friend in Buddy. And every time I donned that black uniform, I suffered guilt, revulsion, and one more truth.

You know that old adage, the one about escaping the frying pan only to find yourself plummeting into the fire.

In the middle of May, weeks after our last heated exchange, I received a text from my brother.

Want to see you, it read.

I anger-texted back, *I don't want to see you*, but smartly stopped myself from pressing the send button and deleted my response. I tossed my phone onto the other side of the bed and attempted to get back to sleep. That, too, got deleted. Groaning, I rolled over and grabbed my phone. I sat up and texted, *When?*

Two hours later, I met Vinnie near the merry-go-round at the same bench where, weeks earlier, I'd hung out with Bo. He sauntered up looking like the Vinnie I knew—a scowl on his face, exhaustion under his eyes, everything in life a burden, a responsibility he wanted to be absolved from.

He gave me a tip of his chin in greeting and then one of those safe, manly hugs that left plenty of distance between fronts and crotches. It was unexpected, more of a show of brotherhood than I'd experienced during the entirety of my banishment to his basement. I suffered another ugly gamut of emotions—regret mixed with resentment along with a liberal dose of relief at seeing him.

When we stood back from each other, he held up his hand. The day pass armband I'd arranged for him at the front gate hung off his wrist. "Thanks for the free admission."

"No sweat. It's good for all the rides. I think you even get a free meal on that level."

"Yeah?"

"The Monster Grilled Cheese is pretty good," I offered.

Vinnie plunked his ass on the bench next to me and looked down at his sneakered feet. I sensed the words he wanted to say but struggled to get out. An awkward silence briefly settled between us.

"How's Lonnie?" I eventually asked.

"Good. He misses you."

I could believe that part. He didn't bother with the fib that Linda did, too, and for that, I respected my older brother. "Do you?" I pressed.

"Yeah," he said, meeting my gaze. I believed him. "You're my kid brother. I'm sorry things went down the way they did. You know I only want the best for you."

"Thanks. I appreciate that."

He nodded, hung his head. "So how are you doing?"

"Great," I said, now the fibber. "Look at me. Don't I look like I'm doing just fine?"

He tipped a glance up. "You look different."

"Oh? How?"

"I've got a buddy at the hospital. Knew him before he went overseas to the desert. He came back. Most of him, anyway. Physically, he returned whole. But not all of him's there. Something's missing. Left behind. That's how you look."

I pondered his words in secret while the robot in charge of my mouth and gestures waved it away. "I'm cool. The job hasn't changed me, just my situation. I've got scratch in the bank, a roof over my head, new wheels—"

"I'm happy about all that," he said. "Just worried about you."

"Don't be."

"I'm your big brother. It's my job."

The robot deactivated. "Your job? Where was all this concern when I was an unwanted guest in your house?"

Vinnie exhaled a sigh, looked away, and shook his head. "We both could have done better, worked harder."

"Could I? Maybe you didn't get the memo, big bro—I was completely destroyed! You're blaming me for everything that happened in the divorce and refuse to believe that Sherry was responsible for any of it!"

"Corey—"

"I'm done being the one at fault! Why don't you break the lockstep thing with Linda and cut me a break? I'm not guilty of the whole world's problems!"I rose and marched away from the bench, my face on fire with rage.

"*Corey.*"

I halted my retreat. Turning around seemed to take far longer than those few seconds. An eternity passed in my estimation.

Again, Vinnie avoided my eyes. "I'm sorry. For all of it."

There was so much I wanted to say to him, to bark at him, all of it angry. But then I recalled what Buddy had said to me on a night weeks in the past about fixing things with Vinnie before they got damaged beyond repair. It was solid advice. I'd be stupid not to follow it.

I slunk back to the bench and sat. Around us, the clank and clamor of the park throbbed—the mad calliope music of the merry-go-round, the shouts of riders on the Dragon Express, and the mixture of laughter and screams from visitors, young and old.

"I'm listening," I said.

Vinnie made a confused gesture with his hands. "Didn't I already say it?"

"Then say it again, this time with adjectives and bullet points."

"I'm sorry."

"For…?"

"For not being a better brother. For not defending you more than I did. Sherry's a jerk."

"So's your wife."

"Hey, that's my wife you're talking about!"

"Am I wrong?"

Vinnie snorted a laugh. "No, you aren't wrong. But I can't go there for obvious reasons. And don't expect me to take your side against her if that ever comes up in front of her."

"Understood."

Vinnie smiled. "So, we good?"

I shrugged. "Eh, satisfactory, at least. You wouldn't believe it, but a friend of mine suggested I reach out to you to fix things even though I'm not the one who broke *this*." I waved a hand back and forth, indicating the two of us.

"Sounds like a smart friend."

"Oh, you have no idea. The smartest. He was all about, 'Corey, you be the bigger man even though you're the little brother.'"

"I'd like to meet him," Vinnie said.

"You would? Come on, then." I stood.

Vinnie followed. A few steps later, he moved beside me. "There's something else. Lonnie's sixth birthday's coming up. We're having a party. I know he'd like it if you were there. Me, too."

"You know I dig my nephew," I said. "But won't it be a little awkward? Me, Linda, in the same room?"

"We're having it in the backyard, so no walls," Vinnie said. "I really want you to be there. You're my only family since Dad passed."

Dad—that was a whole additional conversation, one I was about to broach when Vinnie dropped the last of the day's bombs.

"Just so you know, Sherry'll be there, too. Linda invited her."

I stopped on a dime. "You want me to attend a party that my ex-wife's gonna be at?"

"No, I want you to attend your nephew's sixth birthday. Have some cake and ice cream. Pretend you enjoy the stupid party games like the rest of us. Spend too much on a gift he'll quickly lose interest in. And, if you can manage it, ignore my wife and your ex-wife, who'll be cutting you apart with their eyes from the other side of the yard."

"Thanks. How can I say no?"

"Good."

We resumed walking. For the next few minutes, I forgot about the night shift and the criminal secrets I harbored. We were two brothers together in a normal amusement park where everything cost too much. Kids squealed and ate messy cotton candy. The lemonade was watered down and sour. Bored high school dropouts ran the rides. The only nightmare that would chase visitors home was the rush of riding the roller coaster, that steep plunge downward.

"Where are we going?" Vinnie demanded in his brusque, big brother tone.

"To meet my good friend," I said. And then I made the mistake of pointing at the gothic castle rising directly ahead of us. We were back among the monsters.

Vinnie's face blanched. "Uh, no. No fucking way."

"What?" I got off before he interrupted.

"The Frankenstein Monster? No, just *no*."

"First off, it's *Frelling's*, not Frankenstein's. Second, he isn't a monster. I gave him a name. He's Buddy."

"Buddy?"

"Yeah, and he likes it. I read books to him, eat meals with him. He's great."

Vinnie's eyes snapped fully open. "You're talking about a creature of the night!"

"You work third shift, dude," I huffed. "*You're* a creature of the night. No, I'm talking about a friend. If you want me to come to your stupid birthday party, you can grow a pair and make the effort for me."

We faced off. I softened. "Come on, bro—he's become my best friend."

Vinnie stood rigid. "I knew this was a mistake."

"Mistake? How? What? You coming here?"

"That, you taking a job here, all of it."

"Sorry to be such a disappointment to you. I'm sure Dad would feel the same way."

Neither of us commented after that. The next few seconds dragged out with maddening slowness. Saying nothing, Vinnie resumed walking toward Frelling's Castle. I caught up, took lead, and savored the small victory.

The usual crowd filled the lobby, gawking at posters while waiting for their group's tour inside the theater. Vinnie and I stood among them, arms folded, the defensive language of his body easy to read. After a few minutes, the lobby doors opened and the previous group flocked out, most with shocked expressions on display. Two security guards instructed them toward the exit. The tour guide, I saw, was Martine.

She noticed me and started over. "Hey."

Again, I silently acknowledged her beauty, tired around the edges, and caught myself smiling. "Hey, you."

"What brings you to Frelling's Castle in the daylight?"

I aimed a thumb at Vinnie. "Martine, this is my older brother, Vincent Lowen. Vinnie, this is Martine."

Vinnie warmed and extended his hand. They shook. I could tell that she charmed him, too.

"I was hoping to intro Vinnie to Buddy," I said. "You know, have my brother meet my brother-from-another."

I'd meant it to be light.

"You mean from several mothers," she said. "Go on in. I can put off the next tour for five."

"Thanks—you're the best."

I tipped a look at the two security guards—towering athletes dressed in khakis and black polo shirts, they were nothing compared to the men of Silver Unit who worked the night shift. Both nodded.

We started toward the doors, but I backtracked to Martine. "I bet you wouldn't want to, but any chance you'd like to join me for my nephew's birthday party? There's gonna be cake, ice cream, ex-wives, and dumb party games. Trust me, you'll hate it."

"Sounds hideous," Martine said and smiled. "Worse than partying with the baroness and her brood. But I do love ice cream. Sure."

"See, I told you you'd say no," I said.

"I said yes."

"You did?"

She nodded, flashed another smile at me, and aimed a pointer finger at the open doors. "You'd better hurry. Next performance starts soon."

I gave Vinnie's shoulder a backhand. He followed me past the security guards and through the doors.

"I didn't say you could bring a date," Vinnie grumbled.

"You didn't say I couldn't."

Another small victory, my insides warmed at the idea. It *was* a date, I supposed. Not the kind with a romantic dinner and flowers, but a date nonetheless. My first date in a long time and with a girl I liked. My grin endured halfway down the aisle to the stage where the mad scientist's lab was fully lit up and in complete spectacle. The air reeked of antiseptics and burnt ozone. Electricity crackled between the pair of antennae.

Buddy sat chained upon his bed, head aimed low. My joy shorted out at the image of his defeat. I approached the four stairs to the stage, ignored the warning signs and the alarms that beeped—a quick flip of my ID badge silenced them. I also ignored the danger, which I was quickly reminded of.

Buddy roared and surged up from his crouch toward me. Instead of my good friend, an enraged wild animal jumped at me, with only his chains sparing me the beast's wrath.

I staggered back and into Vinnie, who swore. The angry beast studied me with its one good eye and woke from its rage.

"Corey?" Buddy asked.

I held up my hands in surrender. "Remember me, dude?"

All the energy and menace sagged out of his stare. Buddy retreated to the bed. "Corey, I'm so sorry, so ashamed."

I laughed, my pitch turned up to falsetto. "No worries, brother. Rough day?"

Now it was Buddy's turn to avoid my gaze.

"Hey, pal, like I said, no harm and no foul. I wanted to tell you something. I took your advice. About my brother. And I want you to meet him."

Buddy glanced up and stared at Vinnie, who stood well past the stage and looked ready to bolt from the building.

I tsked at Vinnie. "Get your ass over here."

"No," Vinnie said.

"Remember the deal," I hissed in a whisper.

That got him moving. He made it as far as the steps leading up to the stage but ventured no farther.

"Buddy, this is my brother, Vincent," I said.

Vinnie waved. "Hello."

"Vinnie, this is my friend, Buddy."

Buddy shifted his good eye from Vinnie to me and then he let forth with a sob. Again, I overlooked the danger and crossed the stage to Buddy's cot. I set a hand on his bare shoulder. "What's wrong, pal?"

Buddy peered up. I saw the misery in his expression and worried I'd cry out of sympathy.

"I didn't mean to, I swear, Corey," he said between hitches. "You're my friend. My only friend."

"That makes us even—you're *my* only friend."

He sniffled, got his emotions under control, and set one of his giant hands over mine. I leaned down and hugged him.

At the base of the stairs, Vinnie roostered in place, as though ready to leap into action. "Are you fucking *nutso?*"

I shot him a middle finger.

Buddy drew away. "Your brother Vincent's right, Corey. I'm not worthy of your friendship."

I cast a scowl Vinnie's way. "My brother Vinnie picks his teeth with a steak knife, has holes in his socks because he doesn't cut his toenails before they sharpen into machetes, and pretends to be too tired in order to get out of mowing the lawn."

"Hey!" Vinnie barked. "Why the hate?"

"I'm just pointing out that none of us is perfect. Not him, not me, and not you. But it doesn't stop us from being friends. Or *brothers.*"

Buddy met my gaze. "You consider me a brother?"

"Yeah, I do." I fired another look at Vinnie. "And at the moment, you're my favorite brother."

Vinnie tossed up his hands.

"Do you forgive me, Corey?" Buddy asked.

"Nothing to forgive, really. Like with this bone head," I said, waving at Vinnie, "besides, today's theme is forgiveness."

Buddy flashed a weak smile. "It's very nice to meet you, Vincent Lowen."

Vinnie nodded. "Howdy."

"So what got your shorts twisted in a bunch?" I asked Buddy.

He furrowed his brow.

"What hacked you off?"

"This place, this existence. All day…being gawked at, whispered about, ridiculed. The stink inside this prison cell—I want to breathe fresh air!"

"About that," I said. "I tried to get you a day pass…well, a *night* pass, from the boss. He said no. I'm sorry."

"That you tried is enough," Buddy said. "Thank you, Corey."

"I haven't given up. I'm still working on changing his mind."

"Thank you for thinking enough of me to introduce me to your brother."

"Ain't no thing," I said.

At that point, Martine called down from the open theater doors. "Time's up, Corey. Next show's about to start."

I drew in a deep breath and held it. One more show. Yet another humiliation for my friend, the creature. I returned my hand to his shoulder. "You hang in there, my brother. Remember, you're a Lowen now. You have a solid backbone and can handle just about anything."

"A Lowen? But I'm from Frelling."

"Fuck *Frelling*," I said. "You're pure Lowen, and that makes you more and better than Galabraith Frelling ever was."

Buddy smiled. I extended my fist for a bump. Buddy aimed his knuckles and we knocked.

"I'll see you later tonight. Hang tough 'til then, dude."

Buddy nodded. I tromped down the stairs and smacked Vinnie's breadbasket, shocking him out of his paralysis.

"Bye," he said to Buddy. "Uh, nice meeting you."

Outside, again in the daylight, Vinnie resumed his role as pissed-off, know-it-all big brother. "So, this is your world now, huh? Hanging out with monsters and putting your life at risk?"

I set one hand on my hip and pointed at him with the other. "You're in no position to judge."

"I'm not?"

"Because *you're* the one living with a true monster."

"That's my wife you're talking about—watch it!"

"I'm sure she's terrorized plenty of school kids and given them nightmares."

Vinnie's face morphed into a war mask. I expected him to throw a punch. Instead, he broke up laughing. "She probably has."

"You sure you don't want to stay, grab a bite?" I asked.

"No appetite. You ruined it," Vinnie said.

"Don't you want to take a ride on the roller coaster, see some of the other attractions?"

"No, and I've seen enough. This isn't my scene."

I wasn't sure it was mine. But it had become my world.

I walked Vinnie to the front gate.

"Next Saturday, one o'clock, you know the place," he said.

We performed the ritual of another bro-hug. Vinnie walked through the exit. I watched him go until he was gone from view.

The air rippled with the vibrations of the Hum which I knew originated in the secret chamber beneath the remains of the Great Lakes Monster. On the surface, the day was another late spring beauty. Underneath, the Hum nagged and fondled with its unwanted, unwelcome caresses, reminding me of all the wrongness that lurked below the surface of my surroundings.

I entered the Monsterland gift shop. Anything I purchased here for Lonnie's birthday had a dual appeal—not only would my nephew appreciate it, but his mother would be irate. Win-win, I figured. I moseyed up and down the aisles, perusing stuffed bats and Frankensteins with neon green heads. There were puzzles of the park, pop-up books, and board games. I didn't imagine the official Monsterland board game would get much use or be a hit in my brother's family.

"Hey, Smith," Bo said on my walk up the aisle where tourists could purchase coffee mugs and Monsterland wine glasses.

"Mister Bo," I waved.

I noticed his nostrils flare like those of an angry bull as he snorted out a puff of breath. "So, why are you slumming it on day shift?" he asked.

"Slumming it?"

He flashed a plastic smile. "Yeah, the big, bad Smith from Silver Unit gracing us lowly Monsterlanders with his royal presence?"

I held up both hands in surrender. "There's nothing high and mighty about me, you know that. And trust me, Silver Unit's no better than you, Curtis, or our fellow talent pool from the job fair. Just here to buy my nephew a birthday present."

"May I interest you in a stuffed mummy? Or how about one of those nifty Nestor bathtub toys?"

"I think I'm just gonna go with cash in an envelope."

"You let me down," he said.

"So people keep telling me."

"I thought we were friends!"

The charge caught me completely off guard. Maybe it was because I was already wiped out following my time with Vinnie and Buddy and the fact I should have been in bed, getting ready for the night shift. Friends? I'd never considered us that, but, apparently, Bo had.

"I talked to Ravi about promoting you weeks ago," I said.

"Yeah? And?"

I couldn't repeat verbatim what Ravi had said on the subject. It was too cutting. I couldn't hurt Bo with the truth. Did that mean we were friends?

"Ravi doesn't think you're ready for the night shift."

"And you are?"

"Me?" I laughed. "No, I'm definitely not ready for the night shift."

"Lucky bastard," he growled.

I felt sorry for him, more so because of his naiveté. "Trust me, Bo—you're not missing out on anything. You get to collect a paycheck without worrying about having your throat ripped out. You're in the sunlight, sleep when it's dark, and you don't have to sell your soul for any of it."

He mimed me blathering on with his right hand, making a quacking puppet out of it. "Yeah, and instead of adventure, I get to die of boredom. I want to be where you are, in the action. I *need* that!"

"Raking out mummy tracks and taking a plunge in the icy waters of the Loch Ness Monster tank once every four nights is hardly adventurous. It's shit work."

"Not as shitty as *this*." He held up a pair of Monsterland potholders. Then, tossing them back onto the shelf, he leaned closer. "You got any scoop about that new vampire, the chick?"

Oh, I did. Not that I dared share it with him.

"I know what they're telling people, the spin—another of the baroness's brood captured in a raid. But that's just bullshit, I know it," he said.

I didn't comment and worried that my lack of an answer would become an answer.

"They're saying…"

"Yes?" I invited.

"Her hair and clothes are different, but there's a rumor that she's the one who zapped you in the stones."

"Technically, it was my side."

"Whatever. That's what they say. That they fed her to the baroness when she refused to name names. And that she had help breaking into the park."

I listened, suddenly intrigued. "What do you mean *help*?"

"They say there's this group—enemies of the generals who run this place. The *real* owners."

The Council of Georges, I thought.

"That the chick who zapped you in the peaches—"

"Would you leave my peaches out of it? It was in my side."

"—was one of them, and that she had an accomplice. They tried to blame it on the new hires from the job fair. I'm surprised you didn't get the third degree like the rest of us. Just proves you're one of the lucky ones."

"Yeah, that's me…*lucky.*"

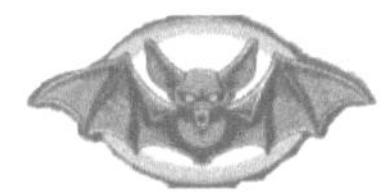

My phone rang. Martine's number came up on the Caller ID. I answered. "Well, hello, you," I said.

"Hey," she said, her voice musical, wonderful. "Busy?"

I glanced around the bungalow's kitchenette. My dinner of Monster Burger and fries with a side salad from the Transylvanian Café sat on the length of counter waiting for me to devour it. "Nothing that can't wait. How are you?"

"Good. Wondering…?"

"Wondering what?"

"This birthday party for your nephew."

"Let me guess—you don't really like ice cream and you were only being nice in front of my brother."

She laughed. "Are you kidding? I *love* ice cream. And I have to be nice five days a week in front of the park's visitors. Screw that the rest of the time."

"Okay."

"It's just that…my kid likes ice cream, too. And he's five."

"Lonnie's gonna be six. Bring him."

"Really?" she asked, the energy in her voice rising. "I didn't want to ask. I mean, that's nervy, right?"

"Very," I said. "And it's also better than okay."

"You sure your brother won't mind?"

"My brother, no. His shrew of a wife…she'll absolutely hate it. But she'll also resent you being there and, most of all, *me* being there."

A brief pause filtered over the phone. "What about you?"

"What about me?"

"Will you mind? I mean, you didn't expect this to be a package deal, right?"

"The more, the merrier. Strength in numbers. Just don't let him get too close to Vinnie's wife, Linda—or my ex-wife, Sherry. They eat little kids."

She laughed. "You sure?"

"That they devour children? I don't have any concrete proof, just a gut feeling."

"No, about me bringing Simon."

"Simon. I like that. His name makes him sound smart."

She giggled again. "I like to think he takes after me and not his father."

"Like I said, Martine, it's fine. I'd love to meet your son. He'll like Lonnie. I like to think that he takes after his dad and not his mother."

"Thanks," she said. "We'll bring a gift."

"You *are* the gift."

We didn't say much more after that. I hung up, ate my dinner and, five hours later, suited up for one more night of service to Monsterland.

I drove the same luxury loaner to a small house one town over from the park. The lawn needed mowing. The small New Englander-style house could have used fresh paint, but the place looked cheery. I got out of the SUV and wandered to the front door. Shades over my eyes, I rang the bell, thinking myself quite cool.

The door opened. The older woman on the other side didn't look impressed.

"Uh, is Martine here?" I asked.

The woman stiffened. "Depends."

"On what?"

"On whether or not you understand the score."

I beamed what must have appeared to be the stupidest of grins. "Not sure the score, because I don't know the rules."

"Then I'll enlighten you," she said. "First, my daughter might be old enough to make her own decisions, but she's still my daughter, so I don't take kindly to anyone hurting her."

"I don't plan to hurt your—"

"I'm not finished. Second, Simon is my grandson. He's not old enough to make his own decisions, but the same threat applies."

"Okay, but it's just cake and ice cream. And a piñata, I think, They decided to not do the bungee jump off a skyscraper."

"Funny man," she said. "Do we understand each other?"

"I think so. I mean, yeah," I said. "Gotta admit, I don't like you, first impressions being what they are, but I respect you for being so protective over your family."

"Good," she said. Stepping aside, she grudgingly welcomed me into the house.

The interior matched the outside. It looked lived-in but comfortably so, and smelled of something delicious baking in the oven—bread or pastry. Framed photographs hung on one wall. Several showed a young girl I assumed was Martine. A green tartan blanket was folded over the back of an overstuffed sofa. Kids toys littered the patch of floor in front of the TV. It was a glimpse into the kind of home I'd never been part of and always longed for.

Martine appeared from a room near the downstairs back of the house. She wore jeans and a light summer top in a pale shade of blue. She looked stunning if a tad stunned. "You're early," she said.

"No rush—just wanted to make sure I had the right address."

She and her mother exchanged looks that were mostly scowls.

"*Simon*," Martine called into the house.

A bedroom door upstairs opened and out bounded the five-year-old. He tromped down the stairs. Simon had dark curls like his mom and wore a smart ensemble of short-sleeved shirt, seersucker shorts, and new kicks. A very stylish young man, I had to admit. He looked at me without any display of worry and extended his hand for me to slap.

"I told you, Simon—I'm not a fan of that!" Martine's mother admonished.

I gently high-fived his hand anyway. "Simon, I presume."

"You would be correct," he said, his tone confident, his vibe one of surety. I didn't like most kids, but I dug this one instantly.

"Do you have the gift?" Martine asked.

Simon skipped into the kitchen, source of that amazing aroma. Martine grabbed her phone, keys, and a tote from the clutter of things atop a hall table. When he returned, the boy carried a present wrapped in blue shiny paper and decorated with a silver bow.

"Well, would you look at that—Lonnie's gonna like you even more than me. And I'm the uncle!"

"It's a race car," Simon said. "One with remote control!"

I patted his shoulder. "Spoiler alert! Though I'm sure his mother's gonna hate it. Well done!"

Martine smiled and kissed her mother. The mom eyed me warily, doing the silent version of two fingers aimed at her eyes and then jabbed knowingly at mine. This interrogation didn't escape Martine's notice. "*Ma*," she huffed.

Her mother feigned surprise. "What?"

"I saw that."

"So long as *he* did," the mom said.

"Oh, I saw it," I said. "Shall we?"

We walked out to my borrowed set of luxury wheels. I reminded Simon to buckle up while we did the same. I adjusted my sunglasses, so cool.

"Sorry about that," Martine apologized.

"Don't be. It's okay."

"It's just that she's overprotective since…" she lowered her voice. "Simon's dad."

"No need to explain. I understand. And I like her. Really, I do."

"Liar," she laughed.

I didn't argue that point. We drove away from the old New Englander where Martine's family lived.

"It's nice having people care about you and guard your back," I said less than a minute later.

"That's how families are supposed to function."

"Yeah, how they're supposed to."

"What about your brother, Vinnie?"

"What about him?" I said lightly.

"Oh. well, he must be proud of you being one of the elite members of Monsterland's night shift."

"The less said about Monsterland today, probably the better," I sighed.

I motored down the road, aware of how pleasant it was to be with Martine and her son. I didn't know if, after today, there'd be a repeat performance, a second date—if that's what this first social outing truly was. But I liked her kid, who hummed to himself in the backseat and fidgeted like a normal five-year-old, and being close to Simon's mother felt somehow right, easy, and joyous.

"So how is life in Silver Unit?" she asked.

I sensed myself readying to answer with a lie and thought better of it. "Pay's great. So are the bennies, like this car and the super-cheap luxury housing," I said. "Only real complaint I have is how much of my soul I've given up to have it."

The tired, worried look returned to her face, and I regretted my confession. "What do you mean?"

I'd revealed too much, too soon. "Nothing. It's just that whole corporate thing, you know."

Martine eyed me from the periphery. We didn't comment on my revelation further and rode in silence for a few minutes, until she again broached the subject of monsters.

"So, tell me about Sherry…"

At that moment, I forgot about the Abyss, the newest addition to the vampire coven, and any worries I had about getting eaten alive by the Loch Ness Monster. *"Sherry,"* I repeated, her name tasting sour on my tongue.

I told her how we'd known each other in high school, hadn't dated then, not until after graduation. Vinnie was seeing Linda Canley, his old high school flame, again after a few years apart. Linda's friend Sherry was interested in me. We went on a double date.

"It was like *The Thing with Two Heads,* now that I think about it," I laughed.

"Which head was Sherry? Ray Milland or Rosey Grier?" Martine asked.

I indulged in a smile. "Well, look at you, Miss Obscure Movie Trivia Expert!"

"I work at a theme park built around real monsters—you'd expect me to be something of a Horror movie buff."

"That was my mom. No soap operas for her, nope—every Saturday, popcorn and her own version of the Creature Double Feature. She had about a hundred of those old movies on VHS. Kept them in a cabinet near the TV. We'd watch two, sometimes three of them together."

"She sounds like quite the hip mom. What's she like?"

"I wish I could remember," I said. "Most days, I can't even recall what she looked like."

"I'm sorry."

"Me, too. We were close, I think. She passed away when I was young."

"And your dad?"

"My dad?" I sighed. "Friday was garbage pickup day. One Saturday morning right after my mom died, I went to the cabinet, hoping to watch two or three of our favorite movies, only to discover that, just the day before, he'd sent them all out to the curb."

Resentment rolled over me. This was starting to feel like another interview for a job with concealed dangers. My dad? I readied to tell her about that day, after I found the cabinet emptied, when the rage filled me and the room shook, how things fell off walls and the beer bottle in his hand shattered, the blood; how, every day after that, he stayed away from the house…no, stayed clear of *me*. How he couldn't stand to be in the same room with me. But then the wise voice in my head realized it was Martine's attempt at understanding the bigger picture because she was interested in it. Interested in *me*.

"He and Vinnie were the team, anyway—thick as thieves. I could never measure up to my brother, the Golden Wonder."

"Silver isn't so bad," she said.

I glanced over. Our gazes briefly connected, and I saw what I hoped was proof of that aforementioned interest. I blinked myself out of the spell before it could take over and returned my attention to the road.

"You know the Great Lakes Monster?" I asked.

"What about it?"

"The Great Lakester has nothing on Sherry Colleen Morrell. She was most definitely the Ray Milland head."

I pulled up to the house. The same sinking emotion pressed down on my shoulders and gut. The last place I wanted to be was here, an unwelcome visitor in hostile territory. The shark cage in Nestor's tank was preferable. But then I remembered my brother's request and my nephew. I reached up and pulled the card from the visor, got out, and waited for Simon and Martine.

"Remember, I've got your back," Martine said in a voice meant only for me.

With those words, most of the gravity lifted off me.

We rounded the house to the backyard where balloons and streamers decorated the patio and a small crowd of parents and kids were gathered. I spotted Sherry instantly, seated in a lawn chair and easy to identify with her platinum hair and sunglasses. My initial shock soon passed. Since our last contact, she'd gained what had to be a solid thirty pounds. She looked pale, frumpy. She didn't have a beer can in her grip, but I feared that was inevitable. My ex-wife pretended to bury her face in her phone screen. We quickly studied one another through the dark lenses of our sunglasses, former opponents sizing up the enemy's condition. I hoped I looked like I'd come out of the last battle intact.

Martine hooked her arm around me. "Introduce us to your nephew," she sang.

Oh, in that moment, I loved her. Even if it was only an act, she'd scored my first victory in a very long and brutal campaign. Beautiful Martine, holding onto me like a devoted girlfriend for the cameras to see, I walked her and Simon over to the picnic table where Lonnie sat snacking on chips and Linda sucked on an invisible lemon.

"Hey, dude," I said to my nephew.

"Uncle Corey," Lonnie greeted. He jumped up and hugged me around the waist.

"Lonnigan, this is my friend Martine and her son, Simon."

Simon held the present in one hand and extended his other for the same greeting he'd used to welcome me. Lonnie slapped palms with him.

"Cool name," Simon said.

Lonnie shrugged. "I think it's Irish."

"Happy birthday—we got you this," Simon continued, extending the gift.

"Wow!" Lonnie exclaimed.

"And I got you *this*," I said and handed him the birthday card.

Lonnie scooped both offerings up and carried them over to a folding card table similarly decorated in streamers and Mylar balloons and stacked with presents. He waved for Simon to join him. I watched Lonnie make introductions to the mostly young boy crowd and few girl guests.

My brother pulled duty at a new grill with all the bells and whistles where burgers and dogs sizzled. Vinnie wore a gray t-shirt and jeans, new kicks, and cool-dude shades. On the exterior, he looked like a man who had it all.

Linda shot me a dirty look. I walked Martine over to Vinnie. We performed another bro-hug.

"You remember my friend, Martine," I said.

Vinnie grinned. "I sure do. A lot better than your other work friend."

Martine laughed. "You mean Frelling's Monster?"

I shook my head.

"Sorry, Frelling's *Creature.*"

"His name's Buddy," I reminded.

"Anyway, glad he brought you and not him," Vinnie said. "Get you a cold one? And by 'cold one,' I mean a soda. The only beer we're serving today is root beer."

"I can do the honor," I said.

I moved to the big cooler set beside the picnic table. Inside, packed in ice, were a few dozen soda cans—no beer or alcohol. I knew why—Sherry. I located two root beers, aware that the disgusted study had shifted from me to Martine. Then I remembered my date was a Monsterlander who gave tours and trained new hires. I figured she could handle the hate from Linda and my ex-wife.

We ate burgers and chips, drank sodas, two figures seated at the outskirts like that table at every wedding reception where they banish all the black sheep. But it was kind of nice.

"So, you're a horror movie junkie?" I said.

"The more horrific, the better," she said. "Though I have a soft spot for the spooky classics. You know, those creature features of which you spoke."

I studied her and the way she sat in a jaunty pose with one leg crossed over the other, the red plastic plate balanced on her slender knee, how she ate that store-bought potato salad without complaint. Martine had exceptional grace.

"Favorites?" I asked.

"Oh, so many to choose from!" she said. If she was aware that we were in the crosshairs from my ex and Vinnie's wife, it didn't affect her. "First, I'd have to say *War of the Gargantuas*—that scene where the Green Gargantua surfaces at the airport and eats the poor woman—"

"Then he spits out her clothes!"

"Right? And I love those two flicks about Majin, the giant statue that comes to life and stomps all the evil soldiers and feudal lords flat in Ancient Japan—*Majin, Monster of Terror* and its sequel, *The Return of Giant Majin*. And don't get me started on *Attack of the Mushroom People!*"

"*I ate the mushrooms!*" I blurted out.

"That's not the exact last line, but close enough," she said laughing. "And a few other rare gems like *Dracula Versus Frankenstein*."

"The one where Dracula has an afro and a Cyclops ring that shoots death rays?"

"That's it!" she exclaimed. "I often think that version of Dracula would be right at home dancing nights away with our baroness. And to this day, I'm still madly in love with Roger Corman's *The Undead*."

I shrugged.

"That's the one where the hooker-with-a-heart-of-gold gets hypnotized and regresses through past lives back to medieval times. Billy Barty plays an imp from Hell who can transform into this bat-thing. I think it's a bat. And you can see the wire! Anyway, it's a tragic black-and-white jewel. Very Shakespearean."

"Sounds it."

"And I love those old ABC Movies of the Week—*The Night Stalker* and *The Night Strangler.*"

"*Heard,*" I said.

"And the one with Kim Darby being tormented by the three little demons. And that one in the Artic where the scientists get trapped with murderous monkeys. What was that one called? *A Cold Night's Death*, I think."

"And don't forget the one with Karen Black and the little devil doll who wields a steak knife and chases her around her apartment!"

She slapped my shoulder. "How could *anyone* forget *Trilogy of Terror*?"

We both laughed. It felt good, pure, *right.*

"What about you?" she asked.

"Oh, I'm completely Old School on that count—the black and white original *Godzilla* with Perry Mason."

"You mean Raymond Burr?" she said, all smiles.

"Yeah, him. Same thing. That movie is my version of the ultimate nightmare—being chased by a giant monster."

"What about Gamera, the giant flying turtle?"

I puffed out a dismissive breath and waved a hand. "I was never young enough for Gamera, the monster that loved little kids. But I can respect the studio's vision. Monsters, even nice ones, are scary."

She toyed with the remains of her potato salad, stabbing at it with the teeth of her plastic fork. "They sure can be."

The light, breezy mood of our discussion altered.

"I'm not afraid of Buddy, because he isn't a monster," I said. "I'm not sure I'm afraid of Baroness von Ullmer any more."

Not looking up, she said, "That's where you're wrong, Corey. You should get more afraid of them, not less. Especially given your duty shift. Fear helps keep you safe."

"I'm more afraid of people than I am of vampires, mummies, and sasquatches," I said. "Ravi Nakur and the people who run Monsterland—the Council of Georges—"

She looked up. "You shouldn't say that name out loud!"

"Why not?"

Martine walked back her surprise and took a moment to compose herself. "You just shouldn't."

"But why?"

"It isn't wise to, that's all. And it isn't smart to ask questions."

"That's the only way to get answers."

"Answers? And what would you do with them?" she asked. "Look, you've got an elite job with great pay and benefits. Do you want to risk it for…*what?* Moral superiority?" She ceased eating.

After a moment, in a much lower voice, I said, "That sixth vampire—you know as well as I do that she's not one of the baroness's old chums."

"I don't know anything about that."

"She's the one who tasered me. They interrogated her and then fed her to the wolves. Or the *bats*, to be specific."

"Where's the proof?" she countered.

"Proof? Tell me what else you know about the Council of Georges—who are they? What else are they hiding?"

She shook her head and laughed. That final bit sounded like surrender, the last gasp from a person before the guillotine's blade slices head from shoulders.

"Time to open presents," Linda announced.

Lonnie tore through brightly papered packages. We all oohed and aahed. He loved Simon's gift. It held top honor until he exhumed his new cell phone—with pre-paid minutes—from his Aunt Sherry. When he opened my card, my nephew feigned passing out, the theatrics generated by the six crisp Benjamins inside.

"One for each year, kid," I said.

Linda wasn't any less hostile toward me after that. Vinnie said I'd set a bad precedent. "Next year, he's gonna expect *seven* large ones."

Sherry only scowled.

We ate cake and ice cream, said our few goodbyes—really only to Lonnie and Vinnie, and started for the car. From the periphery, I saw my ex-wife pursue. At that moment, she seemed more dangerous to me than Uncle Lou or any of his sasquatch kin-folk.

I dug in my soles. "Sherry—"

She wore a counterfeit smile. Martine had gone two steps ahead but turned back, whatever awkwardness between us over our Monsterland debate shelved for the time being.

Her smile tightening, Sherry said, "Sorry, dear, this concerns only my ex-husband."

Martine set a hand on my shoulder. "I don't think so."

"You don't?"

I noted that Simon had halted and backtracked.

"You take Simon to the car," I said to Martine. "I'll meet you in a second."

"Yeah, this won't take long," Sherry grinned.

"You sure?" Martine asked.

"He is, dear," Sherry answered.

I nodded. Reluctantly, Martine walked Simon away. Over her shoulder, she lobbed back, "I'm not your 'dear.'"

As the distance widened, the air between Sherry and I seemed to thicken.

"How could you?" she growled.

"How could I what? Enter this combat zone with a fellow soldier to guard my six?"

Sherry let forth with a humorless cackle. "Do you know how humiliated I am?"

"Humiliated? You?" Now it was my turn to laugh. "You know what? I don't really care how you feel. You're not my burden anymore."

Sherry gasped and covered her heart, as though I'd physically wounded her.

"You made it clear how you felt when *you* walked out on us," I continued. "I've moved on, so get over yourself. Who I see and bring to my brother's house is my concern, not yours." With that, I turned and marched away, feeling not only vindicated but also victorious.

Martine and Simon waited at the car. Saying nothing, Martine raised her right hand for a high-five. I met it. We got in and drove away.

The conversation on the return to Martine's house was airy on the surface—did Simon have a good time? He did. Did he have enough to eat? He didn't. And what did he think of Lonnie?

"He's my richest friend in the world!" Simon exclaimed.

"Yeah, but did you like him?" Martine pressed.

In the backseat, Simon shrugged. "He's okay. He invited me to come over and check out the race car with him."

Martine and I exchanged glances.

"Nice. That'll give me a chance to get to know his mother," Martine said.

I stayed quiet and shook my head. Martine laughed.

I tried not to think of those questions. More so, their answers. Five nights a week from midnight until eight in the morning, I fed and cleaned up after the sasquatch tribe, breathed through my mouth and not my nose, and avoided the deadly grabs of the four imprisoned creatures. I raked Egypt's desert sands while the mummies were permitted to sleep. I spent quality time with Buddy, read to him from whatever paperback novel I remembered to grab, suited up as human bait for Nestor every fourth shift, and helped dole out blood bags to the baroness and her groovy circle. Each night at that point in the work schedule, my guilt deepened and I did my best not to look at the sixth vampire in their enclosure.

Just after sunrise, we jogged to the giant aquarium and entered the secret chamber beneath the Great Lakes Monster's corpse. Urbino snuck off into the room behind the door, and we waited for his return

On May 28, he didn't.

Parsons glanced at his watch. Though he didn't comment, we all understood his concern, because we all felt it. Urbino had vanished behind the security door more than twenty minutes earlier. Rarely was he in there for longer than ten.

As we waited, the unpleasant slither of the Hum made my ears itch and my stomach queasy. I shifted my weight from one booted foot to the other. I had to piss. The long night was nearly over and I was more than ready for it to end. We only needed Knuckles Urbino to reappear to put another duty shift in the books. More money in the bank. More lies and crimes overlooked. More—

Baxter motioned toward the door. "What do we do?"

Parsons maintained a frosty expression. "We wait, as ordered."

"It's been too long," Roman said. "Something's wrong."

Parsons hesitated. He broke protocol and scanned the displays on the work station. Then, grasping that what we all felt could be correct, he approached the door and tapped on the keypad. An intercom activated. "Sir, you okay in there?"

No response came at first. Then a scream tore over the speaker, something alien and angry that certainly wasn't our leader.

"My God," Roman gasped.

"That didn't sound like—" I started.

"We have to help him!" said Baxter.

"You barely managed to touch it," Parsons said. "And I'm ranked at about a quarter of Knuckles's ability to wrangle that thing when it gets bold!"

Information played back and forth in sound bites—so Knuckles Urbino went in there because he'd proven himself capable of grabbing the Abyss with his conscience and putting it to sleep, and none of the others in Silver Unit had anywhere near his ability.

"Uh," I interjected. "The longer we stand here with measuring sticks out, the worse it's gonna be."

Parsons got into my face. "How would you know?"

"You mean about the Abyss? I grabbed onto it, at least for a second or so, the night you dick-heads kidnapped me for my one-on-one with the baroness."

"No, you didn't—I was there!" Parsons barked.

"That's only what the baroness said—to stick it to Ravi. But if you don't want to take my word, I'm fine. I don't even like Urbino."

"This is more than Knuckles," Roman said. "If that thing gets out… I say let him try!"

There I was again, sticking out my neck and unsure of the proper course of action, only going on instinct. In the next second, my pulse caught up to the actual jeopardy. My desire for self-preservation kicked in. I didn't want to go through that door, but I'd already committed. I nodded. Parsons returned to the door controls.

"Whatever you do, don't physically touch the damn thing," he ordered.

"Touch it? Then how am I to—?"

"With your mind, dumb-ass!"

"Oh yeah, right." I sucked down a deep breath and steeled myself for whatever waited beyond that door.

"Stand ready," Parsons said. He keyed in the release. The door opened.

I expected something to rush out, all teeth and tentacles. Nothing did. The outer room was a hub of technology—sensors and gears, lights and power relays. Beyond, I didn't see a single gadget, just a beige room empty and silent save for the Hum.

"Uh," I stammered.

The door closed behind me. I took two tentative steps deeper into the room. Something invisible fluttered near my ears. I stiffened. Where was Urbino?

"*Here I am,*" said a voice that sounded like it was on auto-tune at my back.

I spun around. Urbino stood in the space directly between me and the door. I yelped. He smiled. Indigo light filled his eyes. More of it fizzled out of the scar on his cheek, which had reopened.

"It's my other little friend," Urbino said in the Abyss's deranged child's voice. "Come for a play date."

"We aren't friends," I spat.

"No? But we've spent so much time together, Corey. *Dream-time.*"

"Where is Knuckles? What have you done with him?"

"I'm right here," the Abyss said.

The thing in Knuckles Urbino's body lunged at me. I staggered back. It shoved and I lifted off my feet. Hitting the floor seemed to take longer than it should have. Pain exploded across the back of my shoulders, but I was grateful to finally have made my landing.

Only…

The beige room had altered. I was no longer within the confines of that inner room, but in the open of a place so alien in nature and appearance that I worried I'd struck my head instead of my rhomboid muscles on contact with solid ground. Tall, natural obelisks of black volcanic stone jutted up from the desolate landscape and scraped at a violet-colored sky. A fine mist drifted through the air which turned that purple horizon foggy. Not one but *two* suns hung low in the sky, both distant orbs.

Closer was the cranium-shaped keep-stone I'd envisioned the night Ravi Nakur had me kidnapped from my bungalow as part of my early advanced training. It loomed directly in front of me, moored to the alien landscape. Flashes of indigo light crackled out through the membrane-covered gaps in the stone.

Standing beside that alien brain was Knuckles.

I picked myself up, ignoring the fresh aches, and hustled over to assist Urbino. "Sir, I'm here," I blathered. My voice carried in the air slow and drawn out like words uttered in a dream, a nightmare. I shook him. "I have to get you out of here!"

Urbino stirred and opened his eyes. "Lowen?"

"Give me your hand."

He shook his head. "No, not while it's still *in me!*"

I straightened. "Huh?"

As if on cue, Urbino's cheek scar pulsed. To my rising horror, whatever had burrowed beneath his flesh puffed up, deflated, and wiggled. Urbino screamed. I retched.

Focus, focus, my inner voice demanded. I listened to that verbal bitch-slap and took Urbino's face between my hands. "Use my mind, right?"

I closed my eyes, concentrated.

"It's no good, Corey," the Abyss giggled. "After I'm done with old Knuckles here, I'll make a snack of you."

"Eat this," I said and thought.

I jabbed a mental set of fingers into Urbino's cheek. My supervisor grunted. The thing inside him let forth with the same alien howl we'd heard over the intercom. Urbino jolted and kicked his legs. I wiggled my imaginary fingers in deeper. Something that could have been made of ice or fire stung at my flesh—I couldn't tell which extreme because ice can sometimes burn and contact with fire can make you shiver. Grabbing hold of it proved impossible. Every time I latched on, it retreated deeper.

"Hold still!" I shouted with both my real and imagined voices.

Then Urbino lashed out—in real time, not the airy-fairy version of my imagination. I took the punch to my jaw. It was an awkward uppercut, though quite effective, enough to rattle my teeth. When I opened my eyes, the indigo in his gaze and the mischievous smirk on his lips told me Urbino hadn't socked me, the Abyss had.

"Try that again," the evil child threatened, "and my next love-tap will insure that you never have kids."

"If they're anything like you, good riddance," I said.

I pinned Urbino beneath my weight and attempted to focus: eyes closed, mental abilities sharp, fingertips like metal grips. My consciousness returned to that hated Saturday and the anger that had fueled my shaking of the room.

"Corey," my father called, resurrected by the Abyss. "You know I never really loved you. Not after what you did that Saturday morning."

"Yeah, I know," I snapped, properly pissed. "Now shut up!"

I envisioned my fingers again reaching into the butchered scar on Urbino's cheek. While my physical body restrained the possessed Urbino beneath it, my astral self made a grab. The slimy, elusive son of a bitch bucked against my palm.

"Ow!" I said aloud. "*Ow-wow!*"

Ignoring the sudden discomfort, which I imagined was like shoving damp fingers into a live electrical socket, I pulled back, out from Urbino's massacred cheek. The dark, wiggling thing in my clutches resisted. Urbino screamed. So, too, did the Abyss. Their combined outcries stung at my ear. But I was almost beyond feeling the pain by that point. I howled too, and gave the final yank.

What detached from Urbino's cheek, doing so in a tearing of flesh, resembled a slug—its skin crackling with sparks of indigo light. Urbino went slack beneath me. The obscenity in my hand snapped back and forth, seeking release. I held on.

Now what do I do with it? my inner voice asked. Then it answered, *The cranium!*

I hastened over to the porous stone and extended the horror in my grip through the membrane, back into the dark cavern of the stone shell. As soon as I released it, the Abyss slithered off and out of sight. I huffed a litany of expletives, shook out my hand, and backed away. The alien landscape vanished. I found myself once more fully within that bare, beige chamber.

I opened my eyes and blinked. My right hand was numb. I raised it up, praying it was still there. It was, though my skin looked blue, like it was dead. I flexed my fingers and rolled my wrist. The color surged back. I laughed, the sound a madman's cackle. I aimed my right middle finger in the direction where the alien cranium had been in my vision. And there it was again, only this time real, solid, no figment of a daymare. I squinted and backed away from it. Nothing emerged from the crenulations. The only movement was the undercurrent that stone and its occupant produced. The Monsterland Hum.

I screamed again in a girly falsetto. "Uh, I mean…" My next shout was in a manly baritone.

At that moment, I noticed the room's failsafe lockbox, hanging open on the beige wall. Dangling from a hook was a pair of what appeared to be headphones. I realized I was staring, wondering what good glorified ear buds would be against a horror from the darkest depths of space when I remembered Urbino, on the floor where I'd pinned him. There he was.

Shaking out my hand one last time, I returned to his side. "Knuckles," I called. "Knuckles are you okay?"

He didn't look it. His cheek was a pulpy mess. But at least no indigo gore ran out of it. Urbino stirred, which I took as a good sign.

"*Nuts,*" I huffed.

I grabbed the same hand that the Abyss had driven into my jaw, extended his arm over my shoulder, and performed a decent version of the Fireman's Carry. Urbino was all-muscle, but at that moment he felt like all-cement. I staggered and nearly fell twice on my way back to the security door. There, I hammered on the metal and hoped someone heard me.

"Lowen?" Parsons asked over the intercom.

"Yeah, open up. I've got Knuckles. He's hurt pretty bad."

Nothing happened. Urbino's weight doubled atop my shoulder.

"Did you not hear me?" I spat.

"Is it secured?" Parsons asked.

"The Abyss? Yeah, I sent it back into its shell. Yanked it out of Urbino's face, which is dripping all over me and the floor, so *open up!*"

The door released. I marched through. Roman and Baxter eased Urbino down off my shoulder as the door sealed behind us. Freed from the other man's weight, I rolled my neck and sucked down a deep, cleansing breath.

"That thing was inside his cheek," I said.

Parsons was on the radio. "We have a situation—medical team to the bunker beneath Checkpoint Zero! I repeat…"

Roman glanced my way. "Good job, Lowen."

"No man left behind, right?" I said coolly. I got out one last cackle before the gravity of everything I'd just endured crashed over me harder than Urbino's weight. My legs no longer seemed there. Boneless, I barely made it over to the station's chair set in front of the row of monitors before everything went fuzzy and the ever-present white noise of the Hum shorted out.

When I came out of it, Ravi Nakur was in my face, his sour expression even worse close up. His mop of dark hair was a mess. At first, I wondered if I was still hallucinating. He appeared to be dressed in a men's kimono—pale blue silk with a pattern of Mount Fuji and lotus blossoms.

"Did he get all of it?" Ravi demanded, not to me but one of the shadowy figures working in the background.

"It looks so, yes," a woman answered. I recognized that voice: Doctor Ivy Wandry's. She wore the night-black uniform of Silver Unit. Her glasses and boots lacked all sparkle. I blinked and realized it was quite likely that Ravi had been roused out of his bed according to his man-kimono and slippers, a combination that would have looked comical if not for what I knew the man capable of. I resisted the urge to laugh.

"*Lowen,*" Ravi said.

"Present," I told the school principle.

"Are you sure you sent it back into the keep-stone?"

"That big, ugly rock? Yes. Feel free to go in there and check for yourself if you don't believe me."

Ravi conferred with Parsons.

"All the readouts are functioning in the green," Parsons said in a lowered voice.

Ravi sniffed the air, his focus on me the entire time. "Doctor?"

Doctor Wandry joined him. "I'll need to examine him."

"When you're through, I'll expect a full report."

Roman helped me to stand. I plodded up the stairs, bonked my head again on the low ceiling, swore. Outside, two Monsterland golf carts waited to whisk us away to the first aid station. Roman loaded me into one, while Parsons and Baxter maneuvered Urbino into the other.

The sun was up. The morning air felt warm and smelled fresh, of pine trees and mowed lawns. The first tickle of worry on the other side of one crisis warned me of the start of a new situation.

I'd bested the Abyss. Now Ravi knew the baroness and I had lied about that all-important matter.

I waited in the exam room, shirt stripped off, the time dragging out. Of that latter point, it made sense—Doctor Wandry needed to focus on Urbino's wounds. He was the one who'd been injured in the Abyss's sneak attack. Of the former, at one point I covered my bare nipples with my hands and then felt even stupider and lowered them, puffing out my chest.

The door opened. Doctor Wandry came into the exam room. "How do you feel?" she asked.

"Tired. I could use eight hours of sleep."

"I'll try to get you out of here as fast as I can, but…"

"I still have to make my report. How's Knuckles?"

"Mister Urbino's alive—thanks to you."

I waved a hand in dismissal. "Aw, shucks, weren't nothing!" Man, I'd gotten punchy in the last, dragging hour. I could have slept where I sat, though something told me bedtime was still a long way distant.

She ran through the usual, checking my heart and lungs with the stethoscope, examining my skin. "Four entrance and exit marks," the doctor said. She wanted to know if I tasted anything unusual like bananas or allspice. I told her I didn't know what allspice tasted like—the Abyss, I assumed.

My blood pressure was a little elevated, but she blamed that on White Coat Syndrome—how it goes up when a patient enters the doctor's office due to worry. Otherwise, I was in great shape.

"Try to take it easy and rest," she said. "I'm all set with you. Good work, Corey."

I reached for my uniform shirt. "Does that mean I'm released back into the wild?"

Doctor Wandry's tired smile sagged. "Not yet. Mister Nakur wishes to speak with you."

Even before she was done delivering the news, the door again opened and Ravi strutted in. He'd changed out of his night gear into khakis and black polo shirt, the proper daytime disguise. According to the wall clock, it was after ten. My nerves jolted at his arrival. As tired as I was, I wondered if I'd ever sleep again.

"Thank you, Doctor Wandry," Ravi said.

"Yes, thank you," I echoed.

The doctor flashed a weary smile and closed the door behind her. I suffered Ravi's unwanted stare.

"So, how's Knuckles?"

Ravi didn't answer, only studied me. Then he broke the silence. "Something you wish to share with me, Mister Lowen?"

I shrugged, feigned ignorance. But there was no way to escape those dark eyes and their sharpness. "I just did what I thought was the correct course of action."

"You've lied to me, which is something I can't forgive easily."

"I lied to you?" I snorted as I pulled on my black t-shirt. "Fine. So I can grapple with that monster you've got hidden beneath the park. Instead of getting angry that I kept the secret, you should be overjoyed that you found out. *Yay!*" I tossed up my hands for jazzy effect. "One of your trusted men in Silver Unit stopped that thing from breaking out of its cell."

Ravi grinned, the gesture chilling to behold. "Yes, on that point, I am most delighted. That's been our one weakness on the night shift—men capable of handling the most dangerous of our monsters. But not any more, it would seem."

I avoided Ravi's gaze. "What is that thing?"

"The Abyss?"

I nodded. "When I was in that room behind the door, I saw…I'm not sure what I saw. Only it wasn't…"

"Wasn't Earth? No, what you saw was, I imagine, a snapshot of its planet of origin. What we call the Abyssal, or the Purple World. Not even your coconspirator, the baroness, has been able to identify exactly where that planet exists, how far away. Not that it matters, really. All that does is that the Abyss is here. Crash-landed some eleven years ago. It probably traveled quite a long distance."

"And now that it's here, you've got it locked away underground, powering the entire park."

"Something like that," Ravi said. "The Abyss, when asleep, generates a spectacular energy field."

"The Hum?"

He nodded. "And the least we should do is make use of that power output."

"No, the least you should do is try to communicate with it, figure out what it wants."

Ravi's grin widened. "Oh, that? We already know what it wants. And communicating with it has, already to date, cost the lives of thirty-one men and women. Not to mention those other thousand lost souls. *Eleven years*, Lowen. Does that number have any significance to you?"

The answer sliced through my exhaustion. My eyes snapped fully open. "You mean—?"

"Yes, the Abyss and its keep-stone crashed into Lake Erie the night before the Great Lakester strode out and attacked Cleveland. The Abyss came here to feed. In other words, to eat people."

He said this with a measure of smugness and even laughed.

A parasite living inside the rock which really wasn't a rock but a shell, a carapace, an exoskeleton, a skull. That parasite had created a colossus out of the raw genetic material of anything it collected in the lake—fish, insects, and birds—fusing the biological structure with alien energy, rearranging cells and sizes, and sending it forth to feed.

"The Abyss itself is a non-corporeal entity," Ravi said. "It's more thought than muscle, which is its one vulnerability. Once a night, Urbino or a handful of others enter that room to make sure the Abyss is sleeping, restrained. This is the first incident we've had since—"

"Since the last time it gnawed its way into Urbino's cheek. That scar didn't come from his capture of the baroness, did it?" I interrupted.

Ravi nodded. "So you understand how dangerous this threat is, and the scope of what it is capable of unleashing."

"An alien monster susceptible to hypnotic suggestion," I sighed.

"In that way, we're quite lucky."

I slung my unbuttoned uniform shirt over my shoulder, real cool-like. Only I didn't get beyond that first step before Ravi stopped me in place with a hand on my stomach.

"Not yet, Lowen."

I shuffled back and away from his touch. "It's been an insanely long and trying night, Ravi. Can we do this later?"

"I'm afraid not. With Urbino out of action for now, I've got two capable members in Silver Unit's weekend duty roster of handling any problems that might arise—and one of them wouldn't last very long if that alien nightmare woke up again and decided to go on a snack run. No, I need you to be more present than ever before."

I performed a little dance move and waved my free hand. "*Ta-da!*"

Ravi's grin vanished. "This is serious business. Lowen. You put it to sleep without the use of the neural enhancer."

"That set of headphones in the failsafe lockbox?"

Ravi nodded. "It boosts the mind energy of whoever wears it. You didn't need it to best that alien nightmare. I'm promoting you at once to field supervisor. You'll fill in until Urbino's well enough to return to the job. *If* that ever happens."

My exhaustion surged back, double what it had been. "What? No! I don't want any more responsibility than I've already been handed!"

"You don't have a choice."

I folded my arms. "Don't I? You don't own me, Nakur! I'm an employee, not your slave."

"You're whatever I tell you that you are." He moved in close. I smelled the toothpaste on his breath. *Minty-fresh*, my tired inner jokester remarked. "I can make life for you quite unpleasant going forward."

There it was. The warnings my psyche and the baroness and Buddy had made given substance. A chill sliced me down the middle. All of me froze except my yap. "Don't threaten me, Ravi," it spat.

Several long seconds passed. Ravi's eyes narrowed. "You're an excellent soldier, Lowen," he said.

"Nice to be appreciated."

"So I'm willing to cut you some leeway. What do you want?"

"Huh?"

"To continue in Urbino's shoes. To keep the quality of our staff intact. A nice, fat bonus? Maybe the pink slip to that sweet set of wheels loaned to you?"

I'd already made one deal with the devil. This was just more of me signing my name again in blood. "We're a man short, so how about you promote Wolcotte to Silver Unit?"

Ravi started to argue but instead capitulated. "Done."

"And I want you to approve my earlier request."

"Concerning Frelling's Monster?"

"His name is Buddy. One night—he gets to taste freedom and fresh air."

"Okay. Do we have an agreement?"

"I'm not finished yet, Ravi."

Ravi's smile, so icy, so dangerous, crept wider. "Careful."

"I'll take the bonus *and* that sweet ride's pink slip."

Ravi laughed. My blood turned cold and my bowels clenched at the sound.

The next night, I dressed and proceeded to Checkpoint Zero. Four bodies in crisp black uniforms stood before the remains of the Great Lakester, whose true identity I now knew. Well, according to Ravi Nakur, though I had no reason to disbelieve his explanation.

I strode up to Parsons, Baxter, and Roman. The fourth uniform was tall and appeared to have been shoehorned into his black button down and cargo pants. His boots were as big as watermelons. G.I. Bo saluted.

"At ease, Bo," I said.

"Thanks for the recommendation, Smith," he said, his smile barely wrestled under control.

"You're welcome, and my name's not Smith." I approached Parsons. "You got any problems with this new arrangement?"

"Oh, tons," Parsons said.

"Good. That makes two of us."

"But I couldn't have pulled Urbino out of there like you did except in pieces, so I respect Ravi's decision."

I nodded. "Then also please respect mine. No more frat boy antics with the new guy. I want Bo to understand the dangers before he steps within reach of them. We clear on that point?"

Parsons yessed me. I patted his shoulder and we were off to our first stop.

"They eat people," Parsons warned. "We get in, clean up, dump the Yeti-chow, and get out. No whick-whacking, is that clear?"

Bo listened. Uncle Lou made his usual grab at the last body to exit the enclosure, but we were quicker. We raked the sands of Ancient Egypt. Then it was on to Frelling's Castle.

"I usually take care of Buddy," I said.

"Buddy?" Bo parroted. "Your good pal, the human monster?"

I whirled on him, got right up in his grill. "No one calls him that in Silver Unit. They do, and they're off the team. Ravi listens to me. He has no choice with Urbino down. So let me be clear about it—his name's Buddy and he's no monster."

Bo's throat knotted with what I guessed was quite the dry swallow. "Yes, sir."

I performed one of those head-thrusts at him meant to intimidate. It did. "That's right."

I'd become an asshole, I agreed. But in that moment, I didn't care. We entered the theater. Buddy looked my way. Again, guilt bloomed in my gut. It was like looking at a sad old mutt in a shelter who knows there's little hope of finding a forever home. Or, in Buddy's case, it was because he'd found his forever home, and that place was the worst possible. It was Monsterland.

"Evening, my good man," I called.

Buddy brightened. "Corey!"

We all approached the stage.

"Buddy, say hi to Bo Wolcotte, the new man on the team. He's gonna help us care for your needs from now on."

Bo nervously raised a hand in greeting. Buddy waved.

"And I have some great news for you. I've gotten permission to take you out of here some night. We can ride whatever rides you want, play any of the games, eat whatever you like that they serve in the park—though you might want to steer clear of anything with the word 'fried' in it if your digestive system isn't used to it."

"The fried ice cream's pretty decent," Bo said.

I flashed a smile and a glance through wide eyes that told Bo to zip it without words. When I turned back to Buddy, he was agog with surprise.

"Are you okay, dude?" I asked.

Buddy shifted on his cot. The clink of ankle chains sounded, reminding me that he was still a prisoner despite my good news. "Yes, Corey. I'm just…overwhelmed."

I jumped up the stairs to the stage, aware that I had no fear or worry where Buddy was concerned. "Don't be."

"Corey?"

"Yeah?"

He eyed the others before answering in a soft voice meant only for my ears. "I'm frightened."

"Of the deep-fried ice cream?"

"No, of going out there."

I removed his leg shackles. "Don't be. I'll be there with you the entire time. It'll be fun."

I washed him while the others changed his bed linens.

"What you really need to worry about is your wardrobe," I said. "You don't go out for a night on the town dressed in these shitty PJ bottoms and no shirt. What size waist are you—a forty?"

He shrugged.

"And you gotta sport new kicks."

"Kicks?"

"Sneakers. Footwear. Something really flashy that makes a fly impression, *dawg*." I had him lift up his bare right foot. "What are you, a thirteen?"

I compared my size twelve. His was bigger.

"Jesus, you've got some big-ass feet."

"Technically, they're not mine, they're—"

"Fine, I'll manage."

While he finished dressing, I guess-timated those boats at the size fourteen mark. We exited the small private washroom. Buddy's dinner tray had been delivered. I set him up to eat.

"So when?" he asked.

"I'll let you know as soon as I find out from the powers-that-be. But it's gonna happen, my friend."

Buddy smiled. In that instant, everything I'd suffered through since the day of the job fair proved worth it.

"New guy always gets damp first," Parsons said to Bo. Heeding my earlier advice, he added, "We've got wet suits."

I flashed a grin. Bo suited up and went into the shark cage. Nestor came at him while we vacuumed up the sludge and scrubbed down the tank. We released the half-dozen salmon, and the monster fed. When I pushed the button that lifted the cage out of the tank, Bo let forth with a rousing hoot that echoed over the water.

We entered the mirrored room. I waited near the meal slot for Parsons to present six IV bags of human blood. But what he carried over was a pair of unmarked glass jars filled with dinner for the undead.

"What's this?" I demanded.

"Pig's blood," he answered.

"That's not the deal. Get the real stuff."

Parsons didn't move. "It's all that's in the fridge."

I marched to the refrigerator. Parsons was correct. The only blood products stored inside were identical to the ones he'd first presented. And then the explanation struck me—this was Ravi's doing, part of his punishment to the baroness for her deception regarding the Abyss. I rolled my eyes and approached the slot.

"Baroness," I whispered after opening the small sliding door.

Her voice, sweet and hypnotic, answered. "Yes, Corey?"

I tried to ignore its melody—not easy to accomplish. "I'm sorry. There's been a change in tonight's menu." I handed the first two glass jars through the slot and sensed her disappointment and disgust.

"Mister Urbino's not among you," she said. "Am I to assume that, too, has to do with the change in the banquet?"

"You could say that."

"I'm sorry, too, for you."

She didn't have to explain her sympathy further. She already had on the night I got tested against the Abyss.

"I'll see what I can do," I promised.

I handed four more jars through the slot. Before closing it, I heard lids getting unscrewed. Gone from the view through the two-way mirror was the usual debauched joy from those on the other side, as if to signal the party was over.

At last, we reached our final assignment destination, which was where our duty shift always began. I used my ID to open the door to the secret underground chamber.

"What's this?" Bo asked.

"Don't ask questions," I unintentionally snapped. I hadn't meant to blow him attitude, but it was my first night of entering that other room behind the security door where the Abyss was housed as unit leader—hopefully it was asleep and not looking to feed on human flesh.

I walked in and suffered a flashback. The air smelled like any other dank basement and, for a terrible second, I was back in my brother's rec room. Martine's son sat on the keep-stone in the same clothes he'd worn to my nephew's birthday party. His eyes glowed indigo.

"Hello, Corey," he said in the Abyss's voice.

I stopped well shy of the skull-shaped rock and the monster that inhabited it and folded my arms. "I see I'm gonna again have trouble with you."

"Not necessarily. We could be friends."

"I have friends, thank you."

The Simon-thing laughed. "You don't mean that patchwork oaf made of leftovers, do you?"

"A way better friend than you'd ever be," I said through a taut scowl. "At least Buddy won't try to eat my face."

"His loss. You all taste so finger-licking good!"

"Time for beddy-bye, Junior."

The Simon-thing chuckled. "Tell me a story."

"Once upon a time, a little shit traveled a long distance to make new acquaintances. He wasn't a very good guest, though—tried to devour the locals."

"I asked for a bedtime story, not a biopic," the Abyss said dryly. "And you seem to be under a misconception."

"Am I?"

"About me being young, a child. In truth, I am very, very old." He said this with a glint of malevolence in his eyes and expression.

"Fine, grandpa—it's still time for lights out. Now crawl back into your little keep-stone playpen on your own or I'll shove you the fuck in there."

"You're not afraid of me?"

"Oh, I'm ready to shit my pants over you."

"Not afraid of what I can do? You've seen my other physical identity?"

I aimed a thumb at the ceiling. "You mean that giant, bloated corpse over our heads?"

The Simon-thing's smile widened. "Just because you're able to focus your will into kinetic thought patterns doesn't mean I can't get to you. I'd dug fairly deep into Urbino's meat before you ripped me out."

"I'm about to squash you like a bug and end the threat entirely."

"Better men than you have tried. None of them are alive anymore. *You* kill *me?* That's a joke."

I raised my hand in a threatening gesture. "Smack you into pulp like a fly or mosquito!"

The Simon-thing's smugness deflated. "You? Your own father thought you were a monster. More so, pathetic! Remember when you wanted to try out for soccer after you made the room shake, Corey? Thinking you'd be just like your big brother, Vinnie? A jock the old man could admire and heal what you broke on that ugly Saturday morning? That's a laugh!"

I stepped closer. Then I sensed it was what the little alien puke wanted. I backtracked and closed my eyes.

"*Corey,*" it said in my father's voice.

"Time to go to bed, Dad," I answered.

I imagined grabbing the Simon-thing by the neck of its shirt and guiding it toward one of the holes in the keep-stone. It struggled. I shoved its face through the membrane. The Abyss wiggled and kicked. By the time I'd inserted it down to its shoulders, its body changed into the indigo slug. I dumped it the rest of the way through. No further words were exchanged. I opened my eyes.

The keep-stone hummed and thrummed, but its occupant wasn't anywhere to be seen. I'd wrapped my duties for the night.

Backing away, I greeted the door. I swiped my ID. The door released. I emerged into the power room on the other side, my face soaked in clammy sweat.

"Everything's good," I told Parsons. "We're good."

But it didn't feel that way to me. The night shift ended. On my way back to my bungalow, a single thought pingponged through my head—*I'm going to rid the world of that monster. I'm going to kill the Abyss!*

It again visited me in my sleep, again tried to screw with my mind, this time in the guise of Linda.

"Loser," it/she said, indigo eyes narrowed, blue venom spewing from the corners of its sharp smile.

"Yup, that's me," I said nonplussed and rolled over.

When I woke up in the early afternoon, there was a text on my phone instructing me to report to Human Resources. The same bubbly, chubby girl with dark hair and glasses who always seemed to be on duty handed me an envelope and car keys.

"These are for you," she chirped.

Inside was the transfer of ownership papers to the luxury set of wheels that had previously been a loaner. I thanked her and moseyed out into a chilly, overcast day. A quick check on my bank account showed that Ravi had made good on the other part of my demand. The bonus for saving Urbino's life and untold others from the Abyss was enough that I could put a decent down payment on a house. A rush of warmth powered up from my belly. My own house? After a decade of renting, half a year of squatting in my brother's basement, and two months of living in an upscale, detached hotel room, I was ready. Or I thought I was.

The joy in that way of thinking shorted out, leaving me aware of the bite in the air. Owning a house was a foundation, sure, but one built upon a foundation of secrets, some of them murderous. I gripped the electronic key fob to my new car. It and the bonus had been hush money more than a reward for saving Urbino and stopping the Abyss. That sixth vampire. The truth about the Great Lakester.

I slumped onto the nearest bench and huddled. Sure, I could buy a house. I could pretend to live a normal American life—go to work, earn my paycheck, count the hours until the weekend, come home...but to what?

Approaching footsteps brought me out of the building trance of my thoughts. I looked up to see Martine. We hadn't spoken since the birthday party.

"Hey, I thought that was you," she said.

I stood. She moved closer, enough that I smelled her perfume or body spray. Heavenly distraction.

"Yup, it's me," I said.

"Lousy day, right?"

I shook my head. "Not now. You made it a keeper."

She curled a strand of hair behind one ear. Nervous body language clear, I found it charming. "I wanted to see you."

"Good."

"Remind you how much fun I had, and Simon too at your nephew's birthday party."

"It was a great time. We should do it again. Not at my brother's place, though."

"No, I was thinking…"

I waited for her to finish.

"Mine. Our place. Simon's and mine's. My mom's. Dinner some night?"

"I'd love that," I said.

"My mom will be there, but she'll probably do most of the cooking, which is good, because I suck in the kitchen!"

"I love it less now, but not enough to cancel."

"I'm a lousy cook, in full disclosure."

"Pretty but can't cook? I'll have to reconsider."

"You think I'm pretty?"

The words were out before I could bite them back. "I think you're the prettiest girl I've ever seen."

She looked shocked. Then, saying nothing, she bridged the short distance between us and drew my lips to hers. The kiss was brief but unforgettable. Whatever worries had grabbed me in their clutches vanished. When she pulled away, I was the one shocked.

"Hope that was okay," she said.

I nodded. "Oh, yeah!"

Martine smiled. "Dinner then."

"When?"

She shrugged. "The weekend?"

"Saturday or Sunday?"

"Which works for you?"

"I'm good with either."

"I'll let you know. Oh, and they asked me to work after hours for your little fieldtrip."

"Fieldtrip?" I asked.

"With your friend, Buddy. They asked a bunch of the day workers if they would—at time and a half. I said yes."

"I knew I liked you," I said while, silently, I absorbed this latest intelligence report.

Martine said she had to mosey and that she'd see me Thursday night—and for dinner the following weekend.

"Bye," I said.

Alone once more, it struck me how every time I thought about leaving, Monsterland offered up some new temptation to keep me right where I was.

That afternoon, I registered the car in my name and paid to insure it. I drove to the outlet stores and selected a stylish tracksuit in navy with white details on the chest and a pair of brand name cross trainers in size fourteen. Buddy didn't have a hat head. Even so, I picked up a new baseball cap, the biggest they sold. I drove back to the park. The lot wasn't as crowded as usual given the icy rain that had started prior to my shopping spree. I'd also stopped for pizza and carried the big canvas tote of new purchases and the pizza box through F-Gate and to my little private bungalow.

My plan was to relax, eat a few slices, and scroll through real estate listings on my phone before readying for the night shift. But when I entered Bungalow III, I discovered the place wasn't as private as I'd expected. Ravi sat in the front room, one of the bottles of high-end water from the fridge in hand.

"Lowen," he said.

I snorted, closed the door, and set the pizza box down on the kitchenette's granite counter. "Get you a slice?"

"What kind is it?"

"Anchovies," I lied.

He made a face. "I'll pass."

Good. "To what do I owe this unexpected and, frankly, unwanted visit?"

Ravi grinned and sipped his water. "You know, Lowen, I like you. I never feel that same warmth in return."

I ate a slice of pepperoni without commenting.

"I show you my appreciation, don't I? Time and time again. By now, you've seen the bonus I authorized."

"Thank you," I said. "So why are you here?"

"To inform you that you're all set for a night out with your good friend, the man monster. What is it you call him? Buddy?"

"Thursday night, right?"

Ravi's smile ticked. "News does travel quickly within these walls."

"Some of it," I said.

"Just so you understand, the extra cost for help and added insurance is coming out of your salary."

"I can afford it."

Ravi considered me. "So why don't you like me, Lowen?"

I chewed.

"Even Urbino likes me, and he doesn't care for anyone," Ravi continued.

"The girl from the dumpster," I said while swallowing a mouthful of hard pizza crust. "The sixth vampire in there with the baroness and her flock…what was her name?"

Ravi's smile dropped. "You mean the enemy agent?"

"You had her murdered."

Ravi shrugged. "No, *she* did this to herself. We view her as a threat that had to be eliminated. She was, after all, here to do Monsterland and its mission harm."

"*We*," I stressed. "You mean the Council of Georges?"

Ravi settled back, sipped his water some more, and eyed me above the rim of the bottle. "You've done your homework, Lowen. What do you know about the council?"

"That apparently they can't afford more than one name. And why George? What a boring, tired name."

"George? It's one of nobility."

"It sounds flabby like an old, fat uncle."

"The Council of Georges is named after Saint George, who slew the dragon. Or the *demon*, as it were."

"Well, when you put it that way… Still, it wasn't very saintly of them or you, turning her over to the baroness for dinner. What you did is a crime. You're not above the law."

"The law?" Ravi scoffed. "We *are* the law. Look around you and what do you see? A theme park," he said before I could answer. "Your classic American spectacle—a place for families to ride rides and eat cotton candy and take in a few sideshow oddities. But what we've really done is make the world safe from the monsters that used to prey upon us from the shadows."

"She's still *dead*."

"No, she's undead. And she was a terrorist who could have done untold damage in terms of life and property. She intentionally attempted to cause bodily harm to innocents by releasing Frelling's Creature. *Buddy*. As one of those bodies harmed, surely you see the justification!" His dark gaze drilled into me. I offered no rebuttal or absolution.

"What time Thursday?" I asked.

Ravi snorted again. "You and your friend can have the park as late into the night as you wish—the others in Silver Unit can handle the usual tasks. But I will have sharpshooters stationed and ready to fire if the situation degenerates, and I will expect you to be at the underground bunker below Checkpoint Zero on time to work your usual magic."

"Magic?" I laughed. "Is that what overpowers that ancient evil from the Purple World every night?"

"You mean you haven't figured it out?" he challenged.

"No. Enlighten me."

"It's a combination of strong will being exerted to dominate a being that is, until it exerts its power, only mind, not matter or muscle. You have a very powerful intellect and just enough telepathic and telekinetic might to make it your bitch. And while the Abyss has a taste for human flesh when it's awake in its physical form, it is, basically, afraid of you. You're *its* version of a monster."

With that, he stood and walked out of the bungalow, leaving me alone with cold pizza and the unexpected truth.

I was the horror that hid beneath the Abyss's bed.

I was a monster.

Thursday arrived. The day broke cool and overcast like the two that preceded it. I did my best to maintain a bright expression. Around me, the boxes and garbage bags containing the relics of my past had taken on an even more disheveled appearance. It was time to be a grownup. Right after my night of fun and games with

Buddy and before my dinner date with Martine, Simon, and the scowling matriarch of the family, I'd contact a real estate agent and find myself a new place. My credit score probably wasn't the best, but I had a significant down payment and proof of decent income. Besides, it struck me that apart from the occasional trip to shopping centers or birthday bashes for kids, Monsterland had become my entire world. I ate most of my meals here. I lived here. The line between work and any sort of home life wasn't merely blurred—it had evaporated.

I yanked the tags off the clothes and sneakers, tucked them into a canvas bag, and headed to Checkpoint Zero as usual. No. Not as usual, the park remained lit up and loud. The thumping calliope from the merry-go-round pumped and pounded through the misty night air. Neon lights blazed brightly above my head. A note of something fried in peanut oil drifted on the cool, damp breeze. Until I caught sight of the tank containing the remains of the Great Lakester, I was smiling. It was sort of magical, a realm of wonders, a second chance at experiencing boyhood.

Then I saw those giant, vacant eyes, and I remembered the darker side of being a kid—nightmares and monsters hiding, waiting beneath beds. My boyhood was long over and the monsters were no longer in hiding. In plain sight now, they were in captivity or preserved in a sea of formaldehyde, on display like beakers and body parts in a mad scientist's laboratory.

The men stood at the checkpoint, all dressed in black uniforms. Ravi was the fifth man tonight.

"Getting your hands dirty, eh?" I joked, though the statement traveled far deeper in reality.

"How do you think I made my way to the top? Ten years ago, I started out right where you did emptying the garbage barrels," Ravi said. "I've done every job here that there is to do."

I waved him aside. Ravi strutted over. "Yes?"

"Don't you think it's time to ease up on the baroness? That she and her friends have suffered long enough?"

Ravi chuckled. "Don't tell me that Ursula von Ullmer is your next charity project after tonight's outing with Frelling's Monster? What'll come after that? Nap time with the mummies? A human raw bar for the sasquatches? Or let's all go swimming in Nestor's pool to keep him company?"

"She made a mistake."

"She took a calculated risk and lied to me. I'll decide when she's paid enough for her betrayal, not you."

"You know where all the bodies are buried," I said in a low voice. "So, too, does the baroness. Some of them, anyway. More than a few, I imagine. Strategically, it's better to have her on your side than against you is all I'm saying."

"Go ahead to your friend," Ravi growled. "And remember what I said about sharpshooters."

"How could I forget?" I flashed a fake smile and turned in the direction of Frelling's Castle.

The music continued to pulse, the park to broadcast and exude its façade of happiness deep into the night. On the march to liberate Buddy from his shackles and give him a taste of freedom and fun, it struck me that even if I did put down money on a house, I was trapped here, too. The only difference between my situation and Buddy's or the baroness's was I collected a paycheck. But I was still a prisoner, and Ravi was the merciless warden who held my fate captive.

Two guards dressed in black polo shirts and khakis stood outside the theater doors. I knew they were only for show. The real muscle was hidden in the dark, likely armed with tranquilizer guns and night vision goggles. I gave the men a curt nod and breezed past. On the stage, Buddy stood and paced the limited reach made available by his shackles.

"*Doooood,*" I greeted.

Buddy ceased fidgeting in circles. "Corey? Are we…?"

I shook the bag. "Of course, we are."

I pounded up to the stage and bro-hugged him. Then I emptied the bag of clothes and kicks. Holding up the tracksuit shirt, I asked, "What do you think?"

"I think it's possibly both the ugliest thing I've ever seen and also the most magnificent. I love it!"

"Atta boy. Now, let's get you out of those chains and onto the town for a night of fun," I said. I gripped my ID but hesitated from swiping to release the locks. "Before I do, you should know that Ravi has armed men watching us."

"Of course, he does," Buddy said.

"So that means, you know, we stay in line, don't get too creatively bold. No attempts to shuffle off to Buffalo or skip out on things."

"I won't," he said.

I playfully punched his shoulder and then regretted it after remembering that was where he bore a large surgical scar. "Good. No promises, but if this goes a-okay, I can petition for a repeat performance. Just don't turn into one of those indoor cats who gets out once and then that becomes all it can think about. Trust me, there's nothing out there that's really worth going AWOL over."

"You have my word, Corey," Buddy said, his expression gravely serious.

"I trust you, man," I said.

We high-fived. After that, I told him to get dressed and turned away while Buddy struggled into his new clothes. One of the guards pounded down from the open doors.

"*Hello*—can you give the dude some privacy? *Sheesh*," I said.

The guard carried an ankle monitor, the kind released prisoners still serving sentences at home on lockdown wear. "Ravi says he doesn't leave without this on."

"Oh, does he?" I grabbed the device from the guard's hand and turned around.

Buddy wore the tracksuit and sneakers, and I had to admit I'd done a decent job at shopping. The ensemble fit him well. "How does it look?" he asked.

"*Fly*, my brother. Super fly!" I made the appropriate pimp move with my free hand.

I picked up the baseball cap and tossed on his lid, the bill aimed forward.

"Now, there's only one other bit of bling," I said and lowered to attach the ankle monitor.

Once that detail had been settled, I righted. "Ready?"

Buddy nodded. Together, we walked out of his prison cell to stretch our legs around the vaster cage of Monsterland.

"Shitty weather," I said. "But the company's pretty good."

I noticed the nervous, awkward way he walked. Then I remembered that my friend's entire world for a decade had consisted of the length of his shackles' reach and the small private washroom where he got scrubbed down once a night.

"I think it's beautiful," he said, looking up at the sky with its low ceiling of clouds and around at our surroundings, lit up like a giant chandelier.

I clapped him on the arm. "What are you up for first? Some rides? A snack? You want to shoot some hoops, win a prize?"

"I...I don't know."

"Well, if you want to hit the rides, might not be a wise idea to chow down first."

"Okay."

"But it's your night, pal. You want to load up on fried dough and corn dogs and then hurl it while plunging down the tracks of the Dragon Express, I say let's go for it!"

"I am hungry," Buddy said.

"Then let's eat!"

We started at the concession that sold smash burgers and fries. The black polo shirt manning the place was Carla Gerritt, the older woman I'd trained with during a time that now seemed part of a different life. I introduced them. Carla watched us warily from the cut of her eye as she grilled two burgers, fried fries, and mixed two chocolate shakes. When the food arrived, I splashed a liberal dose of ketchup from one condiment bottle onto my burger and followed with a splash of mustard from another.

"Is that the proper way to enjoy it?" Buddy asked.

"I think so."

He indicated for me to do the same to his burger. I repeated the process then thanked Carla, who hadn't softened one iota, and carried the food over to the line of picnic tables where we two alone would dine.

"You've never eaten a burger before?" I asked.

"I don't think so."

"What about…you know…the dude whose brain you inherited?"

We sat. I realized my question had been not only indelicate but also rude.

"Sorry," I apologized.

Buddy waited for me to distribute the food. "There's no reason to worry. I don't have any of Jim Pollard's memories. The slate was wiped clean."

I passed over his food and shake along with a handful of napkins. "Then you're in for a treat. A messy one."

We ate. The burgers were decent, the fries hot, crisp, and salty. The shake was a perfect compliment. Around us, the park pulsed.

We shot hoops. The black polo shirt behind the counter who handed Buddy the basketball was Curtis Nesbitt the Third, the nerd I'd trained with. He eyed Buddy with a level of wide wonder that could have been awe, fear, or a combination of both.

"You can do this," I said.

Buddy cleared his throat and hesitated. I gave Curtis a tip of the chin. He handed me another basketball. I performed a dribble, the cadence of ball on pavement adding to the night's strange soundtrack, and took my shot.

"Just like that," I said. I'd always been decent at hoops but missed the shot. "Well, not exactly like that," I chuckled.

Buddy dribbled the ball, fired the shot. His nailed the bucket and fed the net with grace.

"A winner!" Curtis said.

The nerd reached up to the prize wall where toys hung in a row and plucked one from its hanger. Extending it toward Buddy, I saw that it was one of the stuffed Frankenstein monster dolls with a neon green face.

"Uh," Curtis said.

But Buddy took it, held the prize against his chest, and thanked Curtis.

"You're welcome, dude," Curtis said.

Music played over the loud speakers—something classic from the '80s. Robbie Dupree crooned *Steal Away* as we approached the Dragon Express where Martine waited to bid us entrance. On this night, there was no line for admission.

"You sure?" I asked Buddy. "I mean, we can start off small with the merry-go-round or the Fear-is Wheel if you want."

"No, I want this one," Buddy said.

I extended a hand for him to board the car.

"You heard the man."

Martine kept to a distance but maintained her diplomatic smile. "Arms and legs are to remain inside at all times," she said. "Stay seated until the car comes to a complete stop and I release the safety bar."

"You're the boss," I said.

She chuckled as I boarded in beside Buddy, the two of us squished up in the front seat. Martine lowered the safety bar and double checked it after it snapped into place. "Enjoy," she said.

Now, it was the band Chicago belting out the tunes as we started our slow drift down the tracks and our ascent back up, higher, higher.

"That lady," Buddy said. "Are you and she…a couple?"

I shrugged. "A couple of what? Not sure. I think we are. I'll know over the weekend."

"She likes you," he said. "I can tell by the way she looks at you."

I puffed up my chest and felt rather grand at that moment. An instant later, we reached the top of the tracks with the night landscape spread out before us—the lights of the theme park and in the distance, those of roads and neighborhoods lit by streetlamps. We appeared to have been transported to the top of one of your loftier metropolitan skyscrapers. The happy emotion continued for another second or two as the car completed its chug higher.

Then it struck me, that downward plunge, and panic jolted me out of my confidence. The bottom dropped out of the world. We raced down, down, down. A high-pitched scream tore at my ear. I confused it for the rush of the wind and then realized it was my own voice. The shred of my conscience not paralyzed corrected course and lowered my octave to a register more manly and appropriate. At something like Mach-100, we shot across the bottom of the track. The Dragon Express performed a roll, leveled off, and raced around a curve, where I promptly deposited my insides.

When I took a break from shouting, I heard another sound at my right—deep guffaws. I turned my head to see my friend smiling widely, expelling belly laughs, the baseball cap gone from his head and sacrificed to the roller coaster gods. I laughed in response. The Dragon Express continued toward the next rise in the tracks, and the same lightness possessed me. Up and then back down, the world raced by me in blurs of light and shadow. The music from the past played around us. For a brief while, I forgot my problems.

The Dragon Express pulled back to its cradle and starting place.

"Who was that up there shrieking their head off?" Martine asked.

I threw Buddy under the bus. "Him."

Buddy laughed. "Again?"

I looked at Martine. "You heard my pal—*again.*"

We rode the roller coaster twice more after that. Lightheaded, I suggested something less gravitational in nature. We hopped on the merry-go-round. Buddy sat astride one of the black steeds with glowing red eyes. I jumped onto the back of a werewolf captured in mid-lope. The dire animals circled at a far slower pace than the Dragon Express, and my thoughts returned to my dilemma.

As Ravi was aware, I knew where some of the bodies were buried, too. Enough of them that, through my silence, I was complicit of the crimes that put them in my purview. After the merry-go-round, Buddy and I ate soft serve ice cream cones— chocolate dipped in luscious fudge. It was a taste from a boyhood lost and falling farther into the past with every second.

"What's wrong, Corey?" Buddy asked.

I glanced up. He had an ice cream mustache and goatee and held his Frankenstein doll against his chest. I wanted to laugh and somewhat did. "Nothing."

"If you're upset, you should tell me. That's what friends do."

I stared at that face, so terrible and also so innocent, with its sticky ice cream disguise. Again, I was reminded of the fact that Buddy—*Frelling's Monster*—had been a better friend than anyone else in my world. Were I to take what I knew about Monsterland to the authorities who might not believe me or, worse, *might* but not act on the information because of greased wheels and palms, that friendship would come to an end. I'd be fired. Likely worse. Ravi hadn't exactly bothered to veil his threats. That was the best case scenario of going against the regime. The worst led to oblivion.

"I'm in a moral dilemma," I said.

Buddy leaned closer, his bad eye hideously large in the glow cast by the nearby merry-go-round. "What about?"

"It's best you don't know," I said. "I wish *I* didn't know. Life would be so much saner."

"You'll do the correct thing. You always do," Buddy said.

This made me smile. What he said wasn't exactly the case, but some of it was true. I liked to think I'd made the correct choices most of the time, which was why I knew I had no other option than to reveal what I knew to the authorities; NDAs and Ravi Nakur be damned. The same curious lightness from the top of the roller coaster before it plunged downward washed over me. Like then, it proved fleeting. I'd lose my job, my hefty salary, and be back where I was before the job fair. I'd probably lose Martine as well as my friendship with Buddy. But I'd reclaim my soul.

"Thank you," I said to him.

"What for?"

"For everything. Dude, you are the best friend anyone could ever hope to have. I mean that." I extended my fist, knuckles aimed his way. Buddy knocked them.

"Come on, let's get you back to your bed—it's been a long night."

We finished our cones on the amble back to Frelling's Castle and crossed the lobby. The two guards I expected to be there weren't. That was my first warning sign, and it triggered instant ice. The second was the red telltale light glowing above the double doors that was normally green. I knew what that light signified—a problem with the exhibit's particular monster. Only in this case, there was no problem, no reason for it to have changed color. Unless—

The doors opened. Standing in the gap was a man dressed in khakis and a black polo shirt. It took me a moment to realize I was facing Curtis Nesbitt the Third, because I was too focused on what he held in his hand—it was the failsafe from the lockbox to be used in a last ditch attempt to contain, subdue, or eradicate the monster.

"Curtis, what—?" I got out before he fired the weapon.

I knew from my months on the job what that gun packed—accelerant and the spark to turn the stream into a high-intensity, portable flamethrower. The fire leapt out of the muzzle in a straight line at Buddy. Horrified, I watched as the lethal furnace struck his chest, and the inferno engulfed him.

"*No!*" I bellowed.

I got one step closer to Buddy, intending to help, though I didn't know how I would, when Buddy let forth with a shriek and, on fire, charged at Curtis. Curtis stepped aside. Buddy plunged through the double doors, his voice lost in the whoosh of flames. Rage replaced horror. Curtis raised the weapon at me. I thought it was a single-dose cartridge, but I couldn't be certain. I halted my advance.

"I wouldn't, Smith," said a voice at my back.

I whirled, and there stood G.I. Bo, who was also armed—his weapon one more suited for fully human targets. "Bo?" I gasped.

Curtis stepped forward and yanked my ID badge off my uniform. He proceeded past me to Bo's side.

"There was more than one of you," I said.

"There were three," Bo said. "But poor Kelsey's now hanging out with Baroness von Ullmer thanks to Ravi."

I moved toward them. Bo held up the gun. Again, I stopped. "I don't know what you want—" I started.

"You've already given it to us. You and your bleeding heart for that collection of spare parts." Bo tipped his chin at the doors beyond the cloud of foul-smelling smoke. "The perfect distraction for us to figure out what the council keeps in that underground vault."

A sudden, Arctic chill tamped down some of my anger's heat. "You don't want to know what's down there, trust me."

"But we don't trust you, so how about you tell us?" Curtis said.

"Death. Destruction. All the ugly D words."

"Disaster?" Curtis added.

"It will be if you go in there. Here's another one—*Don't.*"

Bo's frigid expression lacked all of its former buffoonery. I now faced a true soldier, not one playing dress-up. This brute had flipped the killing switch. "You don't get it."

"Don't I? You're zealots who want to take this place down, release the monsters back into the wild, back under the beds!"

"Is that what Ravi told you?" Bo laughed rigidly. "There are people out there who'd pay a hefty price to know this place's secrets. The competition, Smith!"

I realized my mouth hung open in shock. "So this is all about money?"

"Isn't everything?" Bo asked. He raised the gun. It struck me that I only had seconds left to live.

"What about—?" I blathered.

"The rest of those idiots in Silver Unit? Ravi's sharpshooters? All neutralized," Bo said. "You provided us with the perfect chance to attain our objective with your little night party— and I'm damn good at being a soldier. Ravi should have put me in this uniform long before you got him to."

"Kind of kicking myself at the moment for that," I said.

Bo smirked, took aim. I heard the explosion, but it wasn't the report of the gun. No, the doors to the theater burst open. Something smoldering and hulking stormed through to smash into Bo and Curtis, my would-be killers.

"Buddy!" I cried out.

The shirt had been singed off his chest. So, too, had most of my friend's hair. Clearly burned, he recovered from his awkward cannonball and staggered back to his feet. Bo was back up faster and with greater agility. As I made to disarm him, Bo grabbed my ID badge from Curtis, who was still down and not moving. The gun's report exploded within the tight confines of the castle exhibit's lobby. The glass of the framed poster of Karloff's *Frankenstein* shattered. My injured pal lunged at Bo. Bo screamed and raced out of Frelling's Castle and back into the overcast darkness just before dawn.

I unstuck from my paralysis and moved beside Buddy. He'd been cooked. "How are you, bro?" I asked.

"Fried like our dinner," Buddy wheezed.

"At least you still have that dry sense of humor. Made with real turtles? Come on, let's get you back in bed until I can get first aid out here." I offered my arm.

"What about that man?" He indicated Curtis, who'd been knocked unconscious.

I kicked the flamethrower weapon away from him. And then I kicked Curtis in the junk. Buddy's attacker rolled onto his side, out of the fight.

"I'm not worried about him—it's his partner in crime. He's about to tamper with something so terrible and powerful that it could devastate the entire world!"

Buddy's good eye, its brows and lashes scorched off, narrowed on me without blinking. "Then we must stop him."

"But you're injured."

"I'll be okay. I don't want my friend being hurt. And I've suffered worse pain than this."

Buddy extended his singed knuckles. I knocked them. Together, we ran from Frelling's Castle into the new day's gloom in pursuit of G.I. Bo who was headed to Checkpoint Zero and the Abyss.

The sky had lightened from night's misty darkness, but not by much. The music had ended and, I guessed, the extra workers had departed, leaving only the security team. I tried my radio without much success.

"Silver Unit—Parsons, Roman—does anyone copy?"

The mass of burned flesh at my side staggered and dropped to one knee on the damp pavement. I backtracked and helped Buddy to stand.

"You need to see Doctor Wandry," I said.

"I'm okay."

"No, you're not."

Buddy patted my arm. His touch left a smear of burned skin on the sleeve of my uniform. "If this man does unleash the creature of nightmares, we are all in danger—even the other monsters in this place!"

I nodded. We resumed jogging. We reached the mummy exhibit. A counterfeit Egyptian realm rose at our right. We picked up speed, charged forward and, before us, the destination of Checkpoint Zero appeared.

Three bodies stood or were down just outside the secret door. As we neared, I identified two of them—Roman and Parsons, both on the ground. The one standing over them barking orders was Ravi Nakur. As I identified him, he saw who I was with and raised a lethal dealer of death identical to the one that Bo had carried.

"Lower your weapon!" I shouted.

"But he's—!"

"He's here to help us, and I'd be dead if it wasn't for him. Now lower your gun!" I commanded.

Ravi eyed Buddy before shooting me a look, but he complied. I hastened over to the two fallen men in my unit.

"Stunned—just like you were at the dumpster," Ravi said. "Your good friend Beauregard Wolcotte. This is on you, Lowen!"

"No, it's on you for not doing a better job at background searches. Curtis Nesbitt's in on this, too. He's conked out back at Frelling's Castle."

"That little *shit*," Ravi huffed. "When I get my hands around his scrawny neck…"

"We don't have time for that now. Did Wolcotte enter the security room?"

Ravi's eyes widened. "What?"

"That's their endgame—to learn about your darkest secrets for some competition with deep pockets."

"He can't go in there. IF that thing's awake…!"

I jumped back to my feet and charged at the door, which was closed. I hammered on it once before spinning back to Ravi.

"Wolcotte has my ID badge—give me yours!"

Ravi hesitated. I grabbed it off his uniform and opened the door. I'd made it to the base of the stairs and was inside the secret outer room with its power gauges, all of which jumped madly, before I considered that Bo was armed and I wasn't. I needn't have worried—at least on that one point.

The security door to the keep-stone stood open. A streamer of indigo light pulsed out past the threshold. I swore.

"Is that you, Smith?" a voice asked, one that sounded as if it were made of two—G.I. Bo's and the terrible child's.

"Yes, I've come to tuck you in," I said and silently ordered my feet to move toward the inner room.

The Abyss giggled. "Oh, it's too late for that. I'm wide awake now and ready to leave. And *fuck* am I hungry!"

Swearing again, I marched into the vault. More streamers of indigo flashed around me, their source the lone figure dressed in a black uniform standing with its back to me. As I entered, the figure turned around. It was Bo and, according to the indigo light filling his eyes and dripping out of his mouth, it was also the Abyss.

"Uh," I stammered.

"What's the matter, Smith? Not happy to see me?"

"Frankly, I could do without both of you going forward," I said. "And for the last time, my name's not Smith."

The Abyss smiled widely, so much so that I heard Bo's mouth bones crack through the Hum's pulses. "Too bad."

"Yeah, for you it is, so why don't you be a good little monster and go nigh-nights."

"I don't think so," it said.

And then the Abyss's grin dropped and I was staring at pure malevolence. I would have to attempt to do what I'd already decided. I'd kill the Abyss.

The Bo-thing stepped toward me as I contemplated opening the failsafe lockbox for some added mind-muscle, making that impossible. I remembered what I knew—that the Abyss was afraid of me—and did another of those head-thrusts at it meant to intimidate. Bo shrank back.

"That's right, *beyach!*" I hooted.

Bo straightened. His grin returned. "I see this body isn't much of an advantage…but it *is* tasty."

I readied to close my eyes, reach out with my thoughts, pluck the little fucker from inside the traitorous uniform, and to pop it like a zit when Bo came apart in a shower of indigo light and red blood. Warm, sticky liquid splashed my face. I recoiled, sputtered. When I forced myself to look again, only a human skeleton stood there in the shreds of that uniform. The rest of Beauregard T. Wolcotte had been devoured.

The mess of bones and fabric collapsed. I tracked the indigo glare to the ceiling, where it pooled and then vanished. Above us…

"*The Great Lakester*," I gasped, spitting out the remains of G.I. Bo in a voice barely there.

Overhead, I heard something.

"No, no, *no*," I blathered.

Shaking off, I turned and exited the room and raced up the stairs, again hitting my head on the overhang. "Dammit," I groused on my way up to level ground.

Roman and Parsons were standing thanks to Buddy and Ravi.

"Well?" Ravi demanded.

"Wolcotte's dead."

"Dead?"

"Yeah, eaten alive from the inside out. That thing wolfed him down. He let it loose and it ate him!"

"Didn't you contain it?" Ravi admonished.

"I tried, but the little alien bastard was too quick. It stripped Wolcotte to the bone like a school of piranhas."

"Where is it now?" Ravi demanded.

Mouth hanging open, I shook my head.

We all sort of *turned* at the same time. Maybe we felt that we were being watched. Given the size of those eyes, it was impossible for that crawling sensation to be anything else. As one, we all spun around to see the second of those gargantuan eyes snap fully open. Then both glowed a vibrant purple-blue.

"*Mother*—" Roman huffed.

The rest of us moaned or babbled, paralyzed under the hideous stare of the reanimated giant.

The Great Lakester opened its maw. The powerful beast's roar blasted forth, made worse because the sea of formaldehyde within the tank muffled it.

"How is that possible?" Parsons asked as the bellow faded.

"The Abyss is back in control, making it possible," I said.

"Put it to sleep, Lowen!" Ravi commanded.

I shook my head. "It's too late for that. It's awake and hungry. It's—"

The Great Lakester stirred. It turned onto its stomach, pressed its gigantic hands against the bottom of the aquarium, and pushed up. Its spine met the sealed top of the tank.

"Oh my God," Roman said.

The crunch of buckling metal shuddered through the air. We all backed away.

"Call in the war planes," Parsons said.

Ravi reached for his radio. The top of the aquarium screeched. The colossus pushed harder.

"There's no time," I said. "The only chance we have is for me to kill it."

"You? Kill the Abyss?" Ravi said, again in that dismissive tone.

The aquarium roof heaved.

"Kill it, Lowen—*kill it!*"

The next thirty or so seconds passed in a blur. We ran as the roof of the aquarium cracked open and metal and foul-smelling formaldehyde spilled down. From the cut of my eye, over my shoulder, I watched the behemoth rise up, a giant shadow at our backs.

It let forth with a deafening scream that threatened to freeze me in place. A colossal shattering of glass and the deluge followed as all that formaldehyde was released from confinement. On its heels I heard a loud pop and sizzle, what I would later realize was the power room being flooded. Electricity throughout Monsterland went dark.

Boom

A gigantic footstep sounded at our backs.

Boom

The air turned foul from formaldehyde and the rotting fetor of the monster released from its preservation.

Boom

The ground quaked hard enough to nearly knock me off my feet. The tremor sent Ravi off kilter and into a sprawl. We were all several steps ahead before realizing he'd gone down, and by then the horror was on top of him.

"*Lowen,*" Ravi shrieked.

I stopped, whirled.

Boom!

The giant's head leaned down, dripping slimy gore and formaldehyde and, jaws wide open, it flipped Ravi into its mouth. I heard those sharp teeth crunch bones. Whatever satisfaction I might have enjoyed over Ravi Nakur getting what was due him never manifested. Because I knew I was next.

There stood the Great Lakes Monster, its towering corpse a mess of pickled flesh weeping embalming fluid. It had laid waste to every structure between the aquarium and the merry-go-round.

"*Corey!*" Buddy called.

"I have to try," I said.

"Try what?"

"To kill it."

"How?" Buddy pressed.

"With my mind." I closed my eyes, choked down my terror, and focused. The roar of the reanimated monster attempted to divert me. Still, I conjured the image of its hideous, enormous head, those glowing eyes, and the power source behind them.

Boom

I awaited the thunder of the next footfall, but it never came.

Seems I have your attention, I thought. In my mind, the giant leered hatefully at me through its indigo eyes. I concentrated on those enormous lenses, as I had on Urbino's cheek, and aimed the tips of my fingers up, up.

Contact.

The Great Lakester screamed both in my head and real-time. Ignoring my revulsion, I dug through decayed flesh in search of the alien slug at work behind the scenes.

Come out, damn you, my inner voice shouted. *Where are you, you little bastard?* Something slimy wiggled beneath my projected fingertips. Ignoring the crackles of stinging electricity, I held tight, tighter.

You think you can strong-arm me?

Sure as shit, I'm gonna do worse than just pluck you out of the giant's head! I tugged back.

The Abyss resisted and attempted to slip free. I squeezed tighter. *Let go of me!*

Die, you alien mother!

I'm not afraid of you anymore—you can't stop me! it said in that twisted child's voice and then laughed.

The thing in my grip turned what I assumed was its head and put forth a mouth filled with teeth. Those imaginary fangs chomped down on my imaginary hand. Pain that was nothing but imaginary exploded up my arm. I attempted to squeeze harder, but my grasp was failing.

And the instant I let go, I knew I was dead. The stalled monstrosity would resume its march and I'd follow Ravi into its maw.

The pain's not real, I told myself. *Only a dream. But the Abyss's pain is genuine!* My grip failed. The Abyss had nearly worked itself free of my influence. It laughed around its teeth.

Right as I was about to let go, another hand seized hold of the obsidian and indigo slug.

No, the Abyss screamed. *No!*

That big hand squeezed down. The head of the Abyss puffed up like a balloon clutched at the other end. It attempted to bite, but the most its fang-lined mouth managed was to snap as the fist around it exerted more pressure.

I mentally shook out my massacred hand and reached toward its head. I grabbed hold and choked up. A high-pitched, jarring squeal stung at my ear.

The Abyss exploded in our hands, spraying indigo ichor through our fingers. I wanted to puke. The Hum shorted out. So, too, did the vision. I came out of it to find myself standing beside Buddy, our right hands raised and clasped together.

"That was you?" I gasped.

Buddy nodded. "Couldn't let that thing eat the only friend I've ever had."

I gripped Buddy's hand. We both smiled.

Then we remembered the giant monster.

Slowly, we craned our necks up to face it. The colossus remained standing, swaying unsteadily on its legs, the light gone from its eyes. The Abyss was dead, and with it, the source of energy that had brought the creature back to life.

"Uh," I blathered.

"Corey...*run!*" Buddy shouted.

That got me moving.

We turned and sprinted away. At our backs, the telltale oaken groan of rotting muscle sloughing and decayed bone shattering thundered over the park and numerous alarms, which I hadn't heard until that moment but now screamed around us. Behind us the corpse of the Great Lakester collapsed in a pile of meat and skeletal parts.

We were still running when a black helicopter surged down from the overcast sky and made its first pass over what was left of Monsterland.

I got Buddy over to one of the ambulances dispatched to the scene. They treated his burns. Soldiers with drawn weapons muscled me away. I didn't know it at the moment, but soon after Buddy would vanish from Monsterland. *To a secure location*, one of those uniforms gruffly informed me when I demanded to know.

I stood dazed, disbelieving, the world blurry around me. Voices shouted from somewhere in that fog, sounding like they were at the bottom of a well. A lone figure approached. I assumed it was one of the first responders dispatched to the disaster scene, a uniformed lawman I'd give my statement to.

But through the fog and exhaustion of my shock, I noticed the way it moved—its steps slow, dragging. I blinked, and standing before me was one of the mummies. Stray, the one without an identity, I realized. It moved closer, one arm raised, its desiccated mouth attempting to form words that degenerated into dusty hisses. I didn't speak Ancient Egyptian anyway.

I jolted out of my stupor and backed away. The mummy exhibit had been flattened in the Great Lakester's rampage. So, too, had Frelling's Castle and the sasquatch cage. I didn't know the fate of Big Momma, Big Daddy, Junior, or Uncle Lou, but if people started vanishing in the surrounding communities, we'd know that at least some of them had survived being trampled.

Stray reached for me. In that moment, I understood the mummy's panic, its utter exhaustion. All it wanted was a warm bed and to be left alone to sleep. So sympathetic was I for Stray that my first instinct was to reach out and offer the solace of an embrace.

Then I remembered that Stray was a monster, and I was Silver Unit.

I located one of the big plastic trash bins, removed its garbage bag, and granted respite. Stray crawled into the temporary, makeshift sarcophagus and slumbered while the rest of those who'd survived the disaster assessed damage and picked up the pieces.

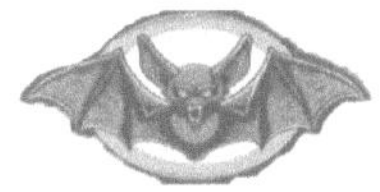

I made it to the bamboo. The turn left was there, in full view. Whatever mystical ward that kept the bungalows hidden had shorted out. I plodded left, past Bungalows I and II, which had both survived the attack. All that remained of Bungalow III was a flattened pile of rubble.

Monsterland was cordoned off, deemed a hazardous waste zone from all that spilled formaldehyde, and given a quite wide berth. Since the only exhibits that hadn't been leveled were Nestor's and the vampire enclosure, a skeleton crew was permitted to work on-site in order to protect their needs and keep them secure. Parsons, Roman, Baxter, and I along with a handful of security guards from the day shift performed our jobs in the desolate remains of the park.

At night, Monsterland had become one gigantic haunted house. Generators kept the juice on for select areas, though the majority of the place brooded in darkness. With the Hum permanently squelched, an unearthly silence hung in the air.

My fellow Silvers and I rarely spoke, which added to the creep factor. We entered the lair of the baroness, distributed blood, fed and cleaned Nestor, and quietly walked out.

One night, we arrived to both exhibits to find them empty. None of the precautions had been triggered. Like Buddy and Stray, Nestor and Baroness von Ullmer and her gang of vampire partygoers were simply gone.

I recharged my phone in my car. My brother had texted and called again. I couldn't speak to him, not then. I dialed the only number I could.

"Corey," Martine said.

For a good five seconds, I forgot how to speak. "Hey," I said.

"Hey."

I instantly sensed the walls she'd tossed around her, invisible but more fortified than those encircling Monsterland. "I'd…I'd love to see you," I said.

"Maybe later," she said, and I knew later meant never. "I'm not in a good place right now. Trying to find a new job. With everything that's happened…"

The sentence went unfinished. Not long after, the call ended.

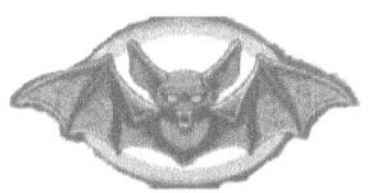

I dreamed about the baroness while slumped behind the wheel of my car, parked alone in the empty lot. With no power and the park deemed unsafe for habitation, I had nowhere else to go after shifts ended. And the last one had wrapped four nights earlier with Ursula von Ullmer's vanishing act.

In the shadows as I slept, six figures crept up to the car, all exuding wisps of mist. I sprang awake but remained frozen in place, paralyzed by sudden fear.

"Yes?" that sixth vampire, the traitorous friend of G.I. Bo and Curtis Nesbitt the Third, pleaded in a juicy voice.

"No, not this one," the baroness said to her coven's dismay.

When the five others hissed, she whipped her head around to face them and all quieted. With the rebellion squashed, she returned to me. I dared not move or breathe. Then, quite tenderly, she leaned down and kissed me, full on the mouth. Cool, she tasted of exotic flowers, her lips soft as petals.

A knock hammered on the door of the SUV and I jumped awake behind the wheel. A gray morning spread beyond the windshield. My mouth tasted like dog food. I needed to shower and shave.

The baroness—had she really been here? According to the signs, day had broken. A somber, late June gray day in which I had no home, no job, no friends, and no clue as to what I'd do next. For the second time in as many months, I'd been destroyed.

Another knock sounded. I yelped and turned toward the window. On the other side was the short, chubby woman with dark hair and glasses from Human Resources, the one who always seemed to be on duty. She wore her usual black polo shirt, khaki slacks, and chipper smile.

"Mister Lowen?" she chirped.

I choked down a dry swallow and winced. Worse, *cat* food. "Yeah?"

"If you'll please follow me…"

Before I could commit or refuse, she started across the empty parking lot. I got out and pursued. A light drizzle fell. I noticed—for the first time—a bird singing from somewhere in the surrounding trees. The Hum, wards, and monsters were gone.

Walking a step behind, I heard her singing a happy little tune to herself.

"Where are we going?"

"To a very important meeting with the council."

"Council? You mean the Council of Georges?"

She didn't answer. We entered through F-Gate, made our way along the thoroughfare where the damage was so clearly presented, and into the HR Building. She extended a hand toward the conference room. My heart attempted to jump into my throat.

No lights were on. I didn't hear the background hum of juice you never acknowledge until the power gets interrupted. I opened the door and entered.

Four figures sat around the conference table, each seated in those miserable chairs. It could have been the day's gloom mixed with the lack of lighting or something else, but I swore all were encased in medieval armor—helmets, chest plates, the whole deal.

"Well," I said.

Suzy Sunshine entered behind me and took a fifth chair at the head of the table. "Please close the door, Mister Lowen, and be seated."

I remained standing. "What is this about?"

"Your job," she said.

"Job? The job's gone. Monsterland's no more."

Her smile endured, and it struck me that, all along, the receptionist guarding that desk was the real power in charge, the head of the Council of Georges.

"Some of our attractions have been relocated temporarily, including your pal Buddy. And there are other monsters out there, Mister Lowen," she said. "And, of course, we intend to rebuild. But in order to do that, we need the right people on our team. With Ravi Nakur regrettably dead, we're searching for the best candidate to run operations."

Her smile evaporated, and she stared right into me.

"What do you say to another promotion, Mister Lowen?"

The idiot in control of my mouth answered, "What kind of salary and benefits we talking here?"

THE END

<u>**About the Author**</u>

Raised on a healthy diet of creature double features and classic SF TV, **Gregory L. Norris** writes regularly for numerous short story anthologies, national magazines, novels, and the occasional episode for TV or film. Gregory novelized the NBC Made-for-TV classic by Gerry Anderson, *The Day After Tomorrow: Into Infinity* (as well as a sequel and a forthcoming third entry into the franchise for Anderson Entertainment in the U.K.), a movie he watched as an eleven-year-old sitting cross-legged on the living room floor of the enchanted cottage where he grew up. Gregory won HM in the 2016 Roswell Awards in Short SF Writing and was a 2022 Finalist. He once worked as a screenwriter on two episodes of Paramount's *Star Trek: Voyager*. Kate Mulgrew, *Voyager*'s "Captain Janeway," blurbed his book of short stories and novellas, *The Fierce and Unforgiving Muse*, stating, "In my seven years on *Voyager*, I don't think I've met a writer more capable of writing such a book—and writing it so beautifully."

In late 2019, Gregory sold an option on his modern Noir feature film screenplay, *Amandine*, to the new Hollywood production company Snarkhunter LLC, owned by actor Dan Lench, a devotee of Gregory's writing. In late 2020, Snarkhunter optioned Gregory's tetralogy Horror film based upon four of his short stories, *Ride Along*.

Twice Norris has been nominated for the Pushcart Prize. He is the author of the novel *Ex Marks the Spot* (Woodhall Press) and the forthcoming release of SF tales of wonder and adventure stretching from Sol to Pluto, *The Solar System* (September 2022), and a delightfully dark dystopian novel, *The Lost City of Books*. In 2023, Van Velzer Press published his hilarious paranormal novel, *Desperate Housewolves* and will follow *Monsterland* in 2025 with *Kindred Spirits: Gothic Gay Romance Stories*.

Gregory lives and writes at Xanadu, a century-old house perched on a hill in New Hampshire's North Country with spectacular mountain views, with his rescue cat and emerald-eyed muse.

Follow his literary adventures at:
http://www.gregorylnorrisauthor.com/

Other Van Velzer books by Gregory Norris

The Lost City of Books

A Dream Within A Dream

Desperate Housewolves

Coming in 2025 …

Kindred Spirits: Gothic Gay Romance Stories

Love Books?

SUPPORT AUTHORS – buy directly from
independent publishers. This puts more royalty dollars into the
pockets of your favorite author – and gives them time to write
their next book.

Visit us for links to our other books as well as many other
vibrant publishing companies to
find the book for you.

Send a note to join our **Book Launch List.**

Director@vanvelzerpress.com

These ARE The Books You've Been Looking For.

Vanvelzerpress.com

www.ingramcontent.com/pod-product-compliance
Lightning Source LLC
Chambersburg PA
CBHW060716190726
48289CB00002B/706